FAR OUT
FAIRY TALES

STONE ARCH BOOKS
a capstone imprint

INTRODUCING...

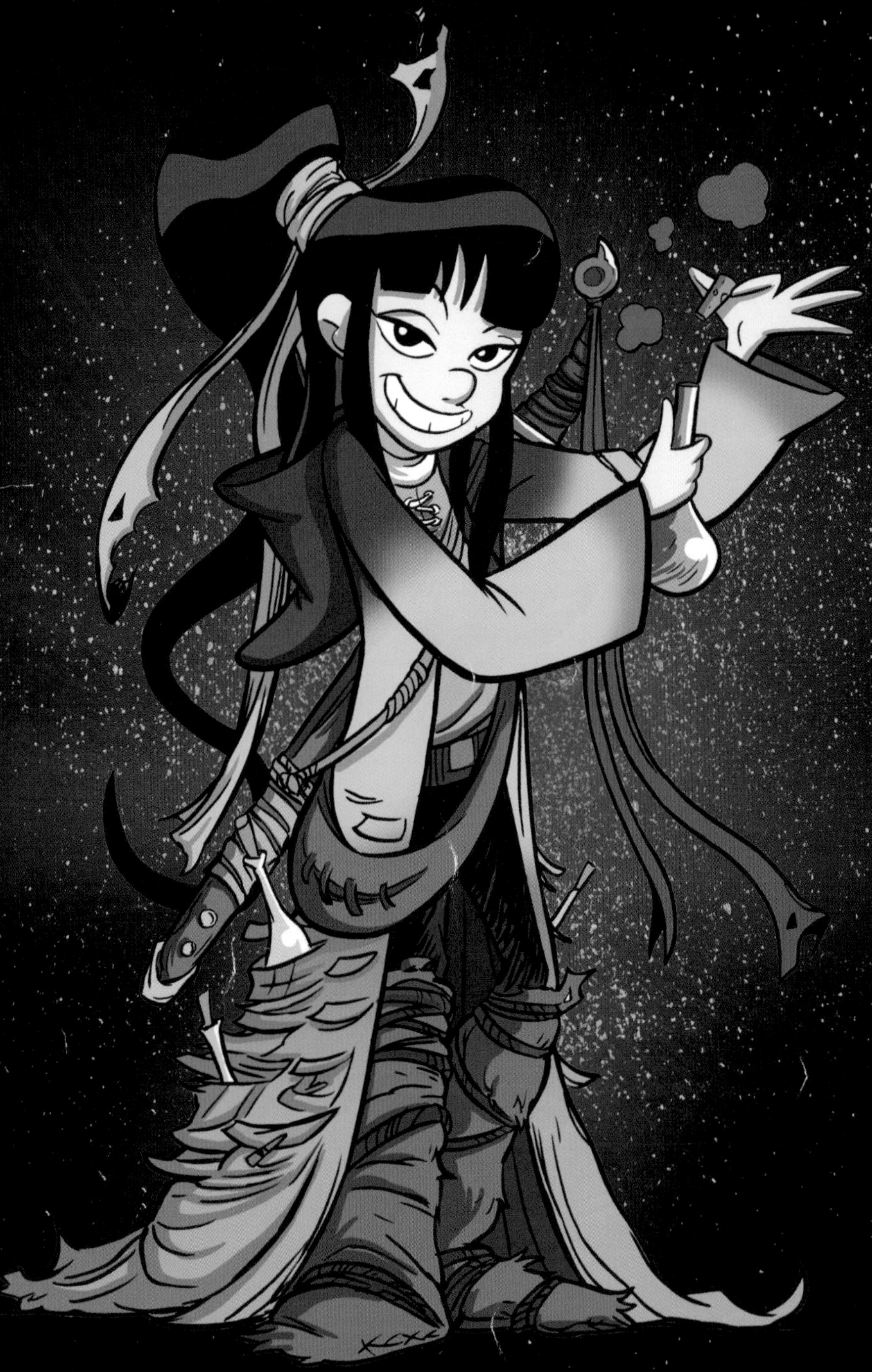

AURORA

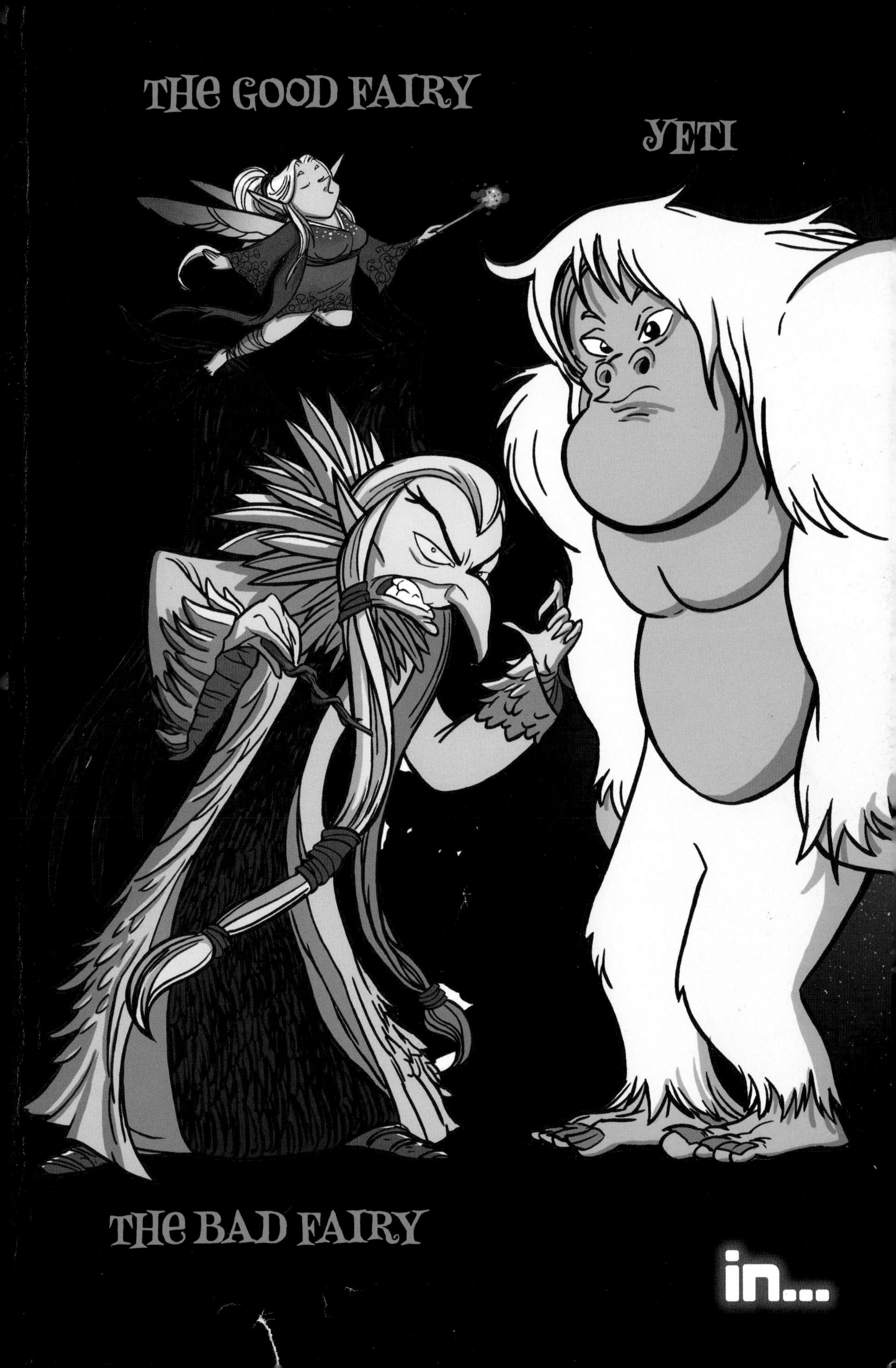
THE GOOD FAIRY
YETI
THE BAD FAIRY
in...

Far Out Fairy Tales is published by
Stone Arch Books
A Capstone Imprint
1710 Roe Crest Drive
North Mankato, Minnesota 56003
www.mycapstone.com

Cataloging-in-Publication Data is
available at the Library of Congress
website.
ISBN 978-1-4965-3784-3 (hardcover)
ISBN 978-1-4965-3786-7 (paperback)
ISBN 978-1-4965-3788-1 (eBook PDF)

Summary: In a faraway land, a princess
named Aurora lives in a castle...
honing her magic amid a slumbering
kingdom! To save her subjects, Aurora
must concoct a potion made of
the rarest ingredients. Can Aurora
succeed in her epic quest, or will the
kingdom--and she--be doomed
to doze forever?

Designed by Hilary Wacholz
Edited by Abby Huff
Lettering by Jaymes Reed

Printed and bound in USA.
009673F16

SLEEPING BEAUTY, Magic Master

A GRAPHIC NOVEL

BY STEPHANIE TRUE PETERS

ILLUSTRATED BY ALEX LOPEZ

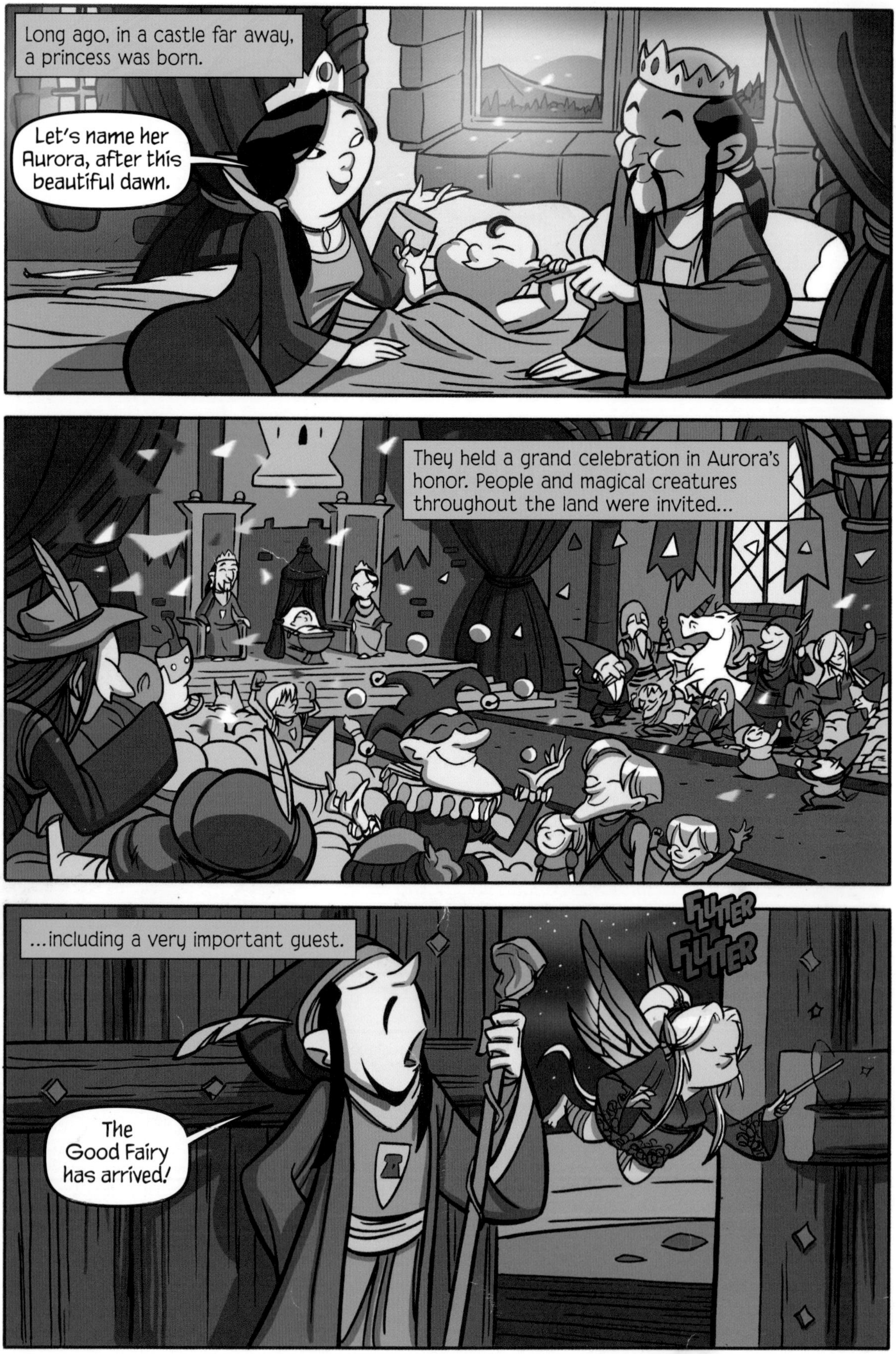
Long ago, in a castle far away, a princess was born.
Let's name her Aurora, after this beautiful dawn.
They held a grand celebration in Aurora's honor. People and magical creatures throughout the land were invited...
...including a very important guest.
FLUTTER FLUTTER
The Good Fairy has arrived!

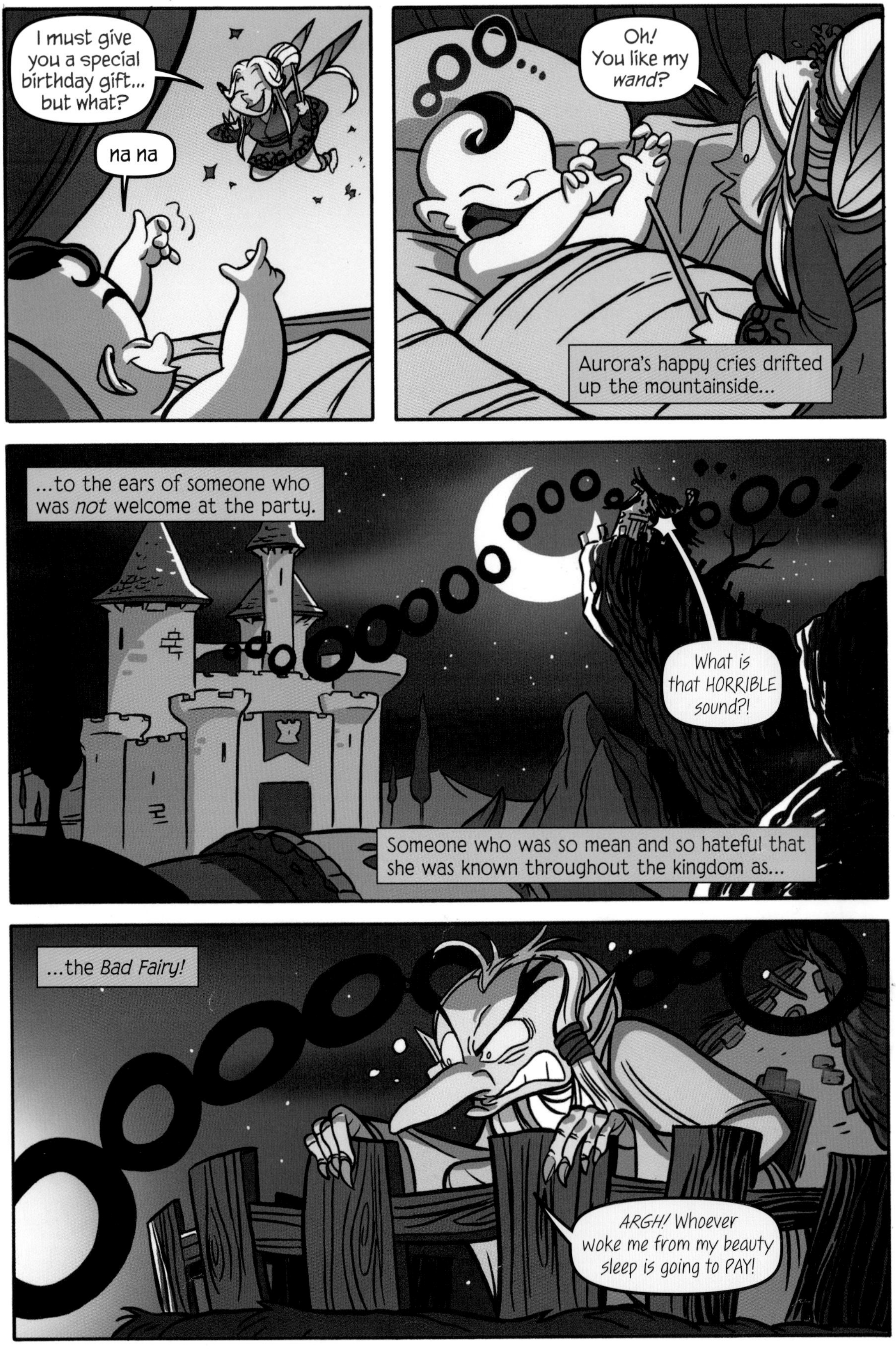
I must give you a special birthday gift... but what?
na na
Oh! You like my *wand?*
Aurora's happy cries drifted up the mountainside...
...to the ears of someone who was *not* welcome at the party.
What is that HORRIBLE sound?!
Someone who was so mean and so hateful that she was known throughout the kingdom as...
...the *Bad Fairy!*
ARGH! Whoever woke me from my beauty sleep is going to PAY!

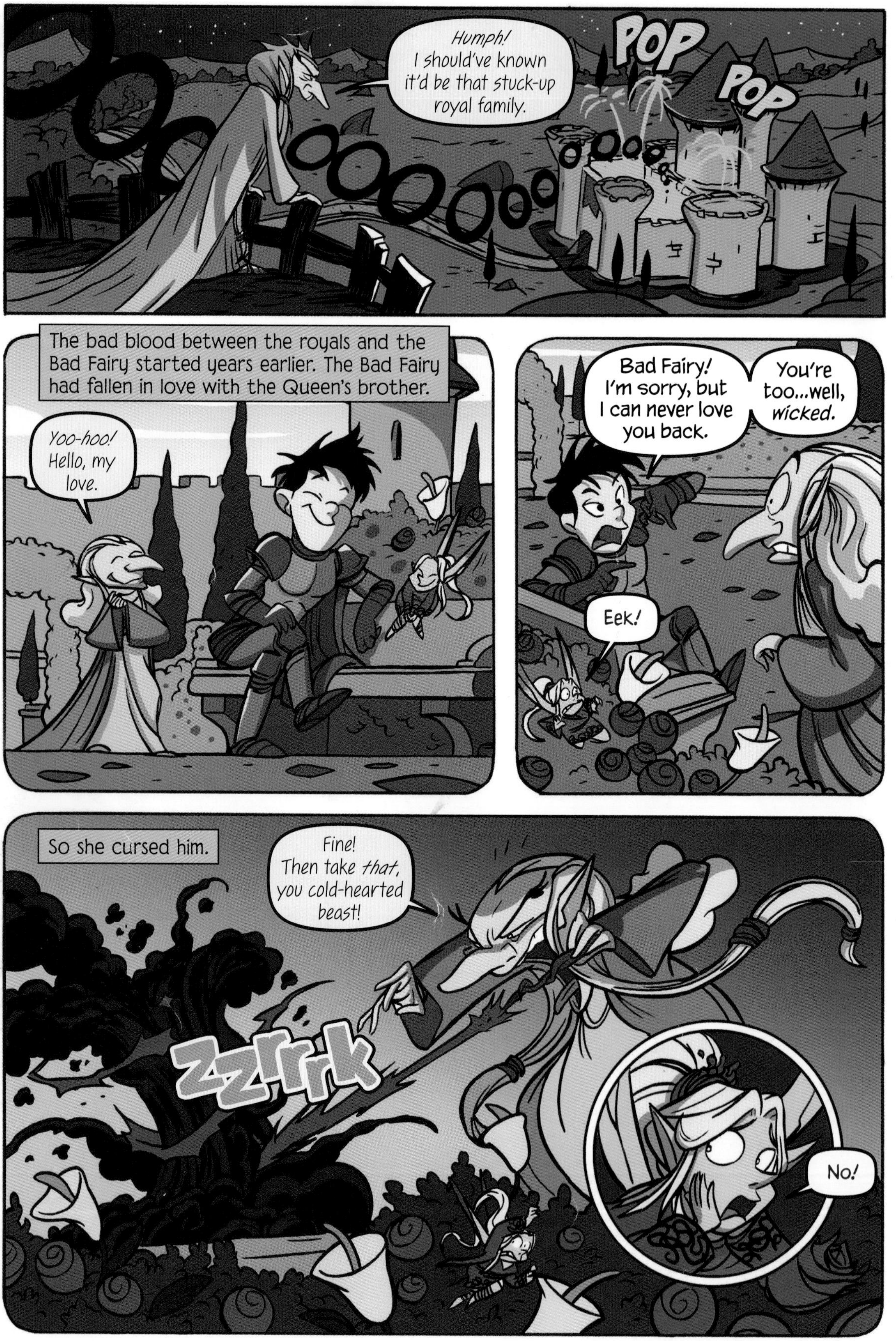
Humph! I should've known it'd be that stuck-up royal family.
POP
POP
The bad blood between the royals and the Bad Fairy started years earlier. The Bad Fairy had fallen in love with the Queen's brother.
Yoo-hoo! Hello, my love.
Bad Fairy! I'm sorry, but I can never love you back.
You're too...well, *wicked.*
Eek!
So she cursed him.
Fine! Then take *that,* you cold-hearted beast!
ZZrrrk
No!

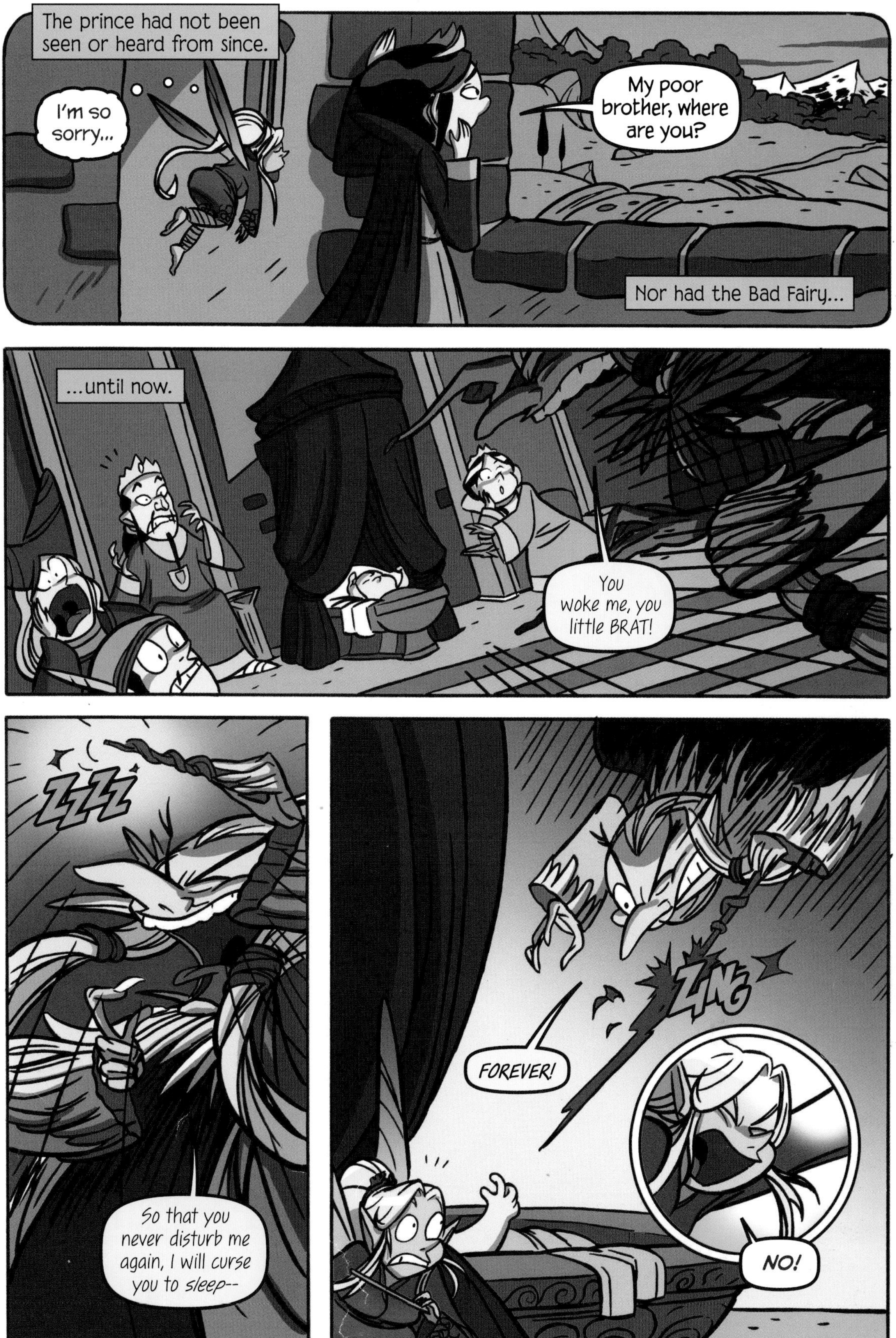
The prince had not been seen or heard from since.
I'm so sorry...
My poor brother, where are you?
Nor had the Bad Fairy...
...until now.
You woke me, you little BRAT!
ZZZZ
So that you never disturb me again, I will curse you to *sleep*--
ZING
FOREVER!
NO!

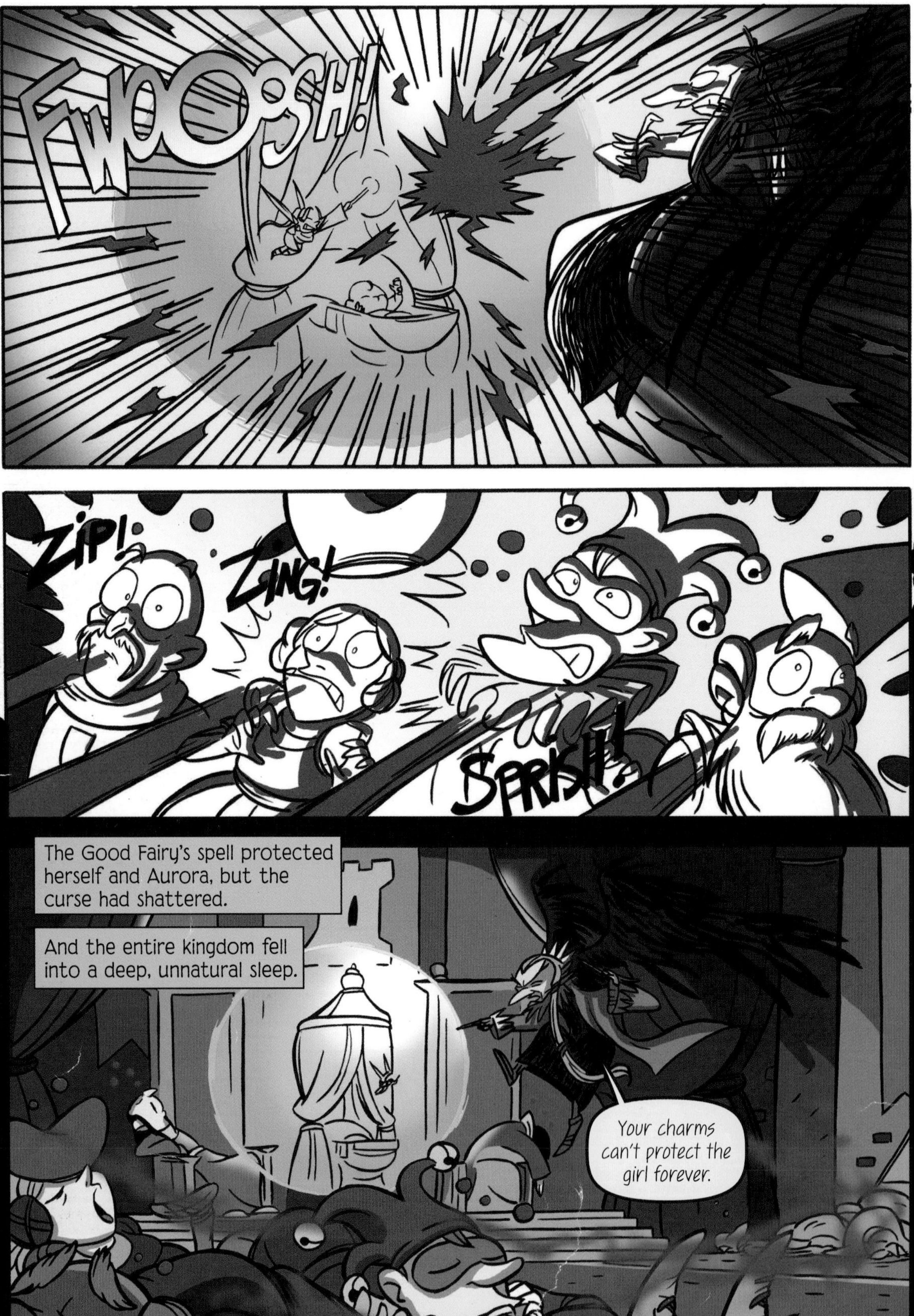
FWOOSH!
ZIP!
ZING!
SPRISH!
The Good Fairy's spell protected herself and Aurora, but the curse had shattered.
And the entire kingdom fell into a deep, unnatural sleep.
Your charms can't protect the girl forever.

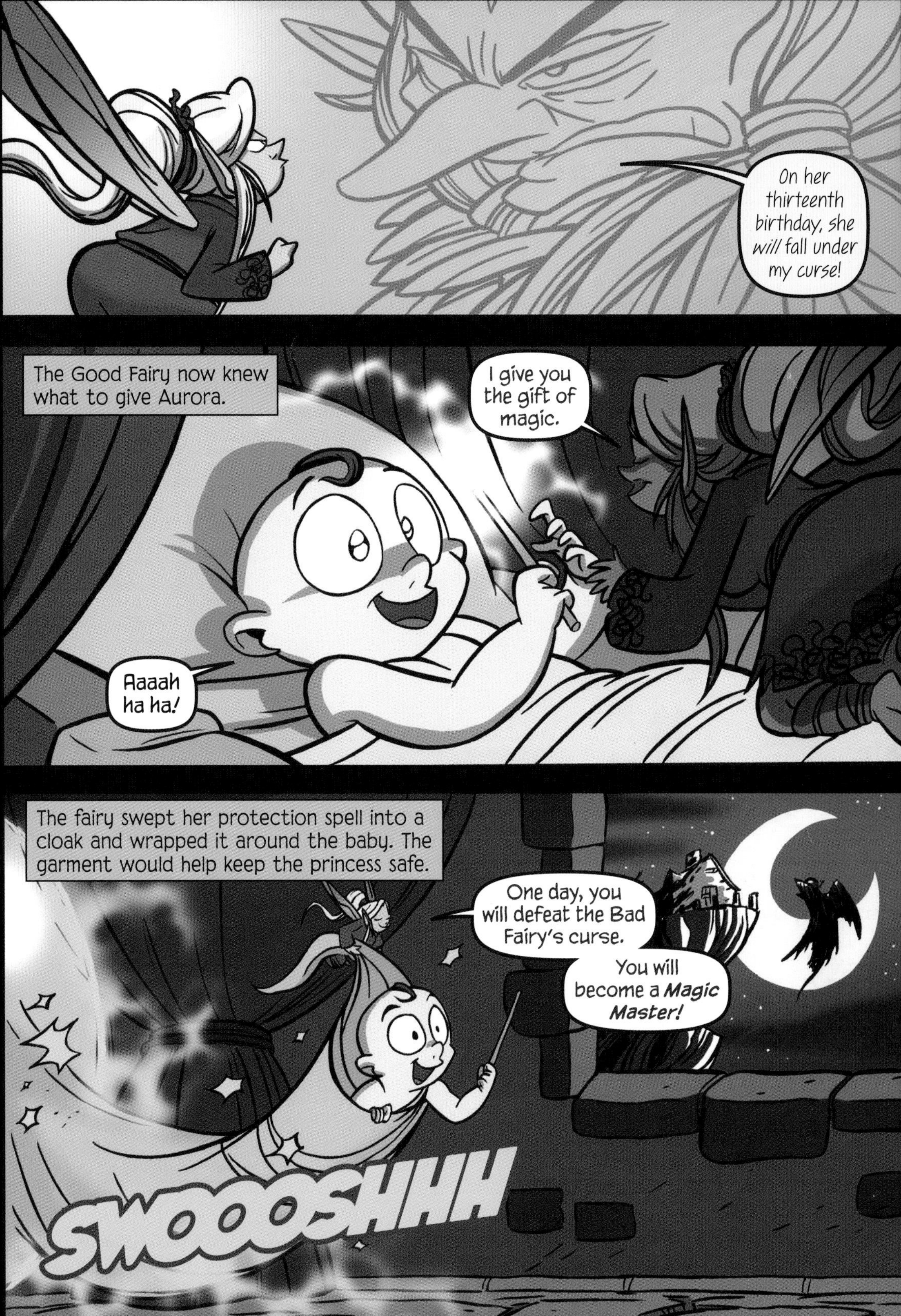
On her thirteenth birthday, she *will* fall under my curse!
The Good Fairy now knew what to give Aurora.
I give you the gift of magic.
Aaaah ha ha!
The fairy swept her protection spell into a cloak and wrapped it around the baby. The garment would help keep the princess safe.
One day, you will defeat the Bad Fairy's curse.
You will become a *Magic Master!*
SWOOOSHHH

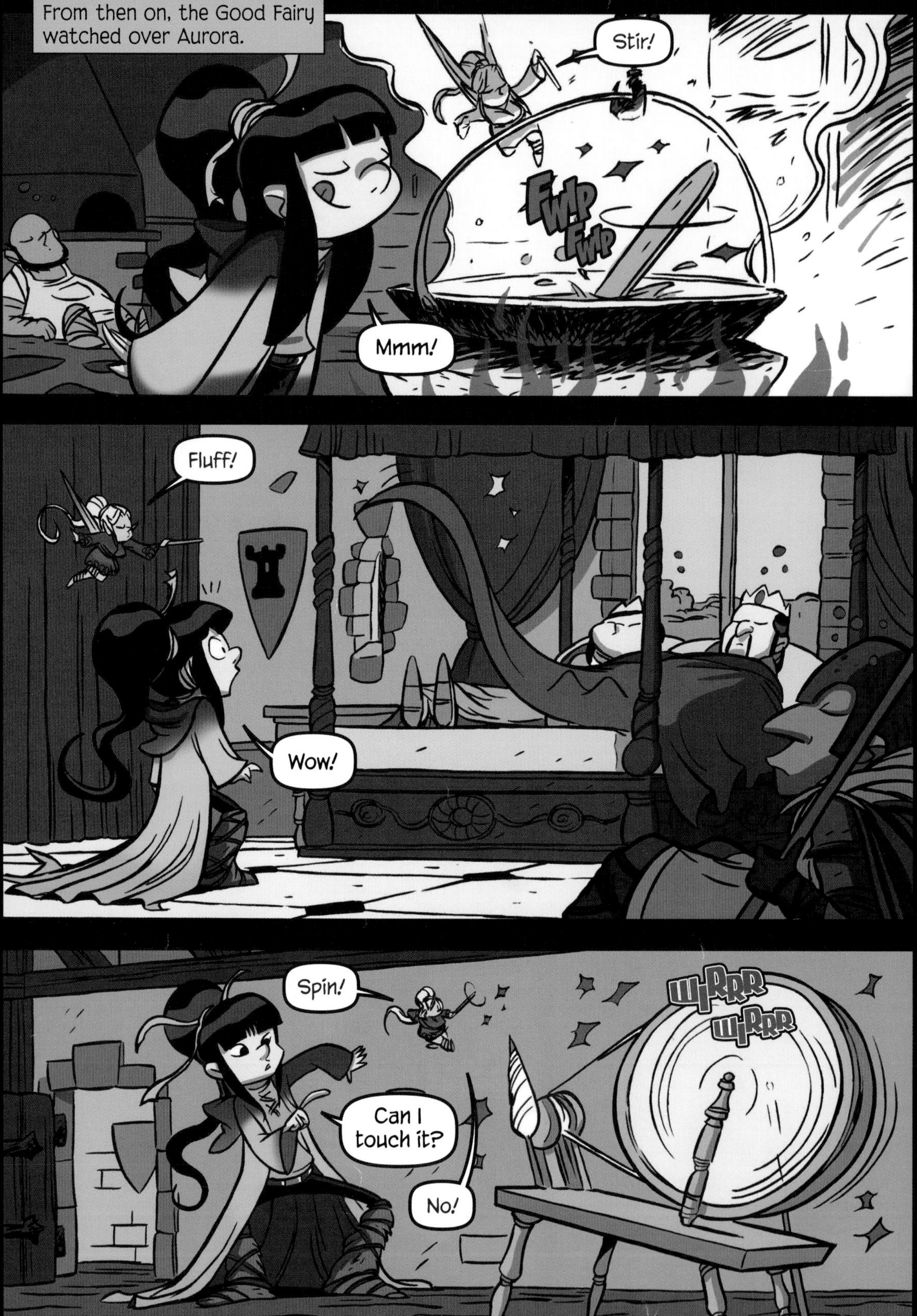
From then on, the Good Fairy watched over Aurora.
Stir!
FWIP FWIP
Mmm!
Fluff!
Wow!
Spin!
WIRRR WIRRR
Can I touch it?
No!

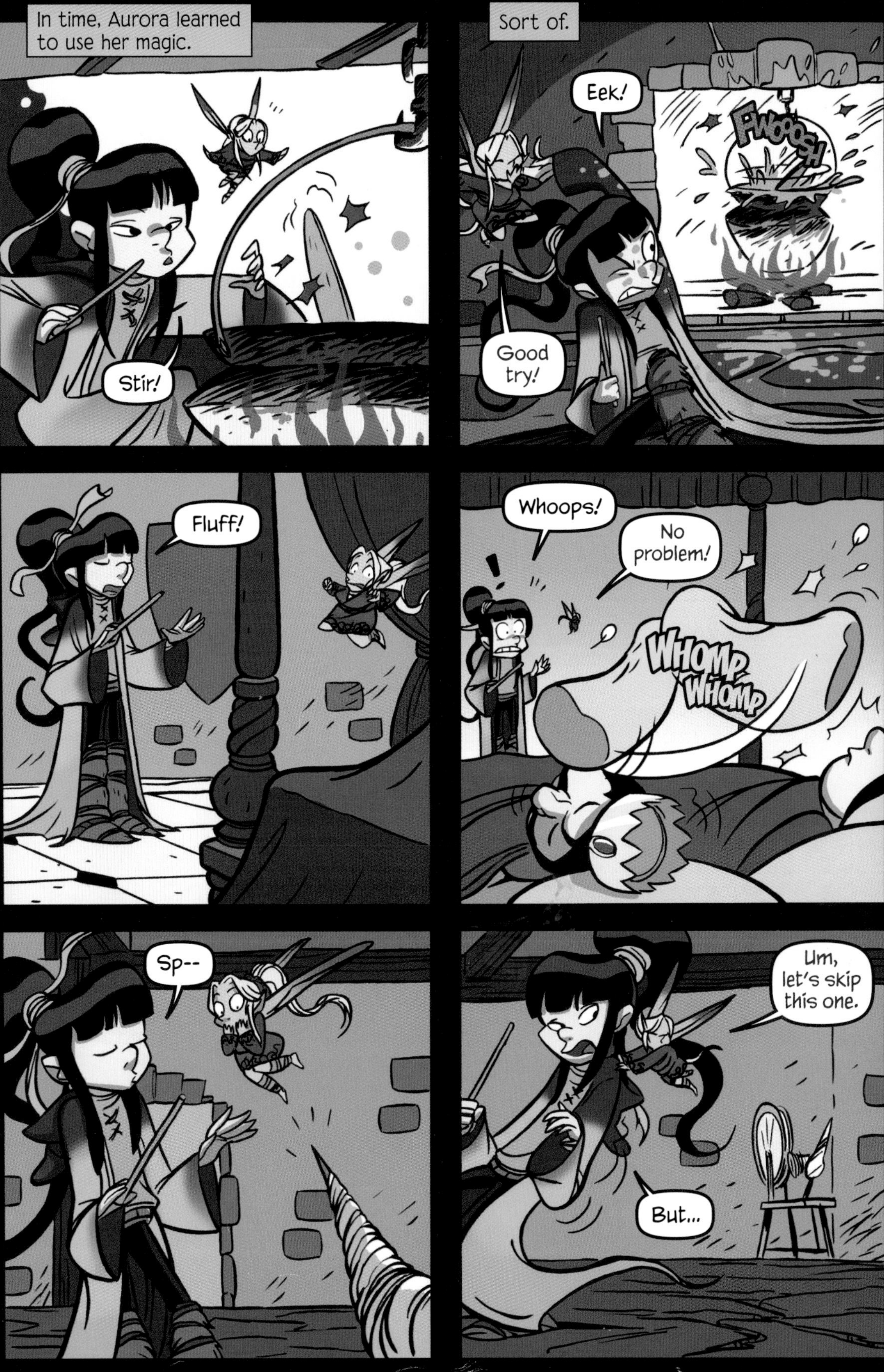
In time, Aurora learned to use her magic.
Stir!
Sort of.
Eek!
FWOOOSH
Good try!
Fluff!
Whoops!
No problem!
WHOMP WHOMP
Sp--
Um, let's skip this one.
But...

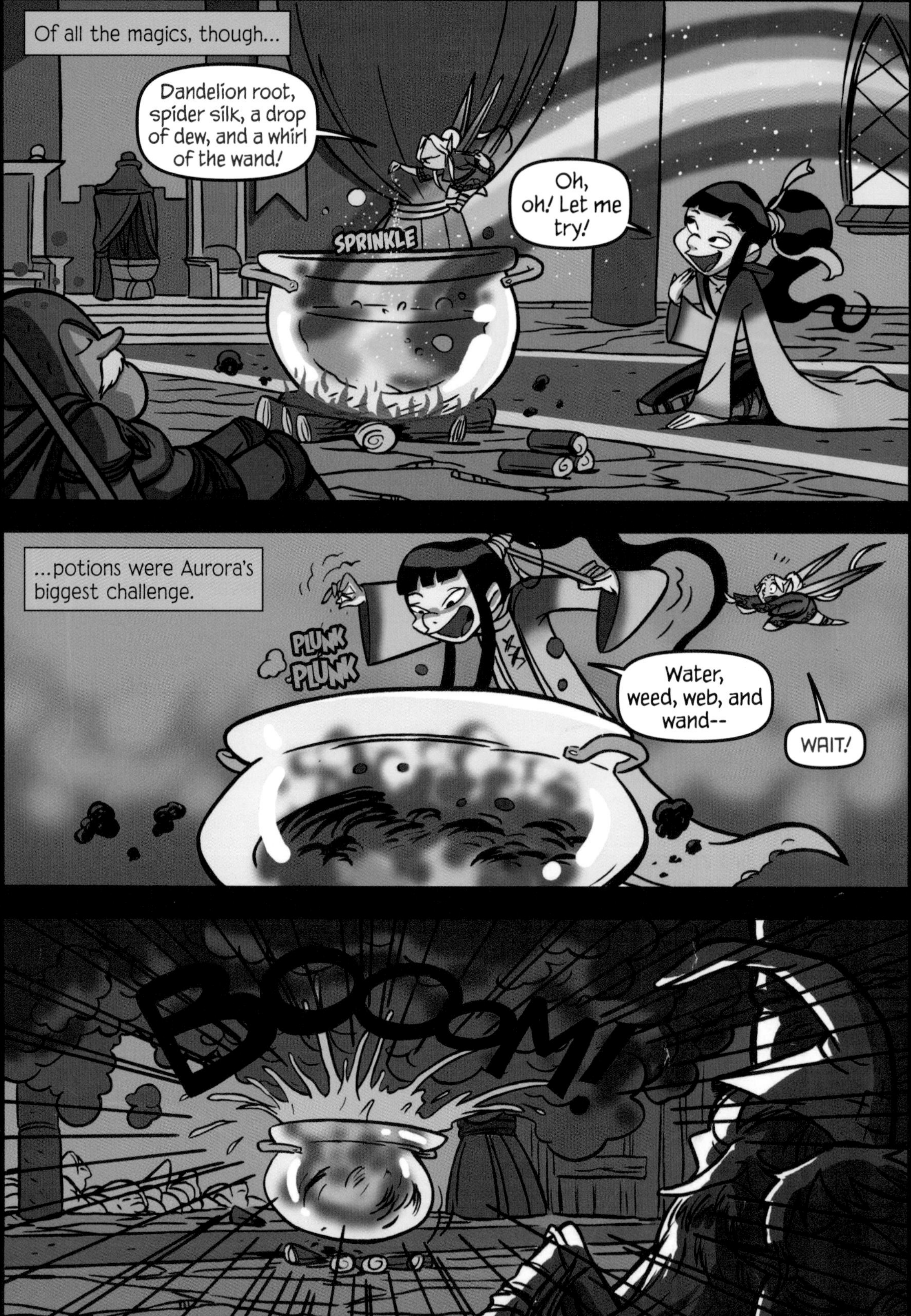

Of all the magics, though...
Dandelion root, spider silk, a drop of dew, and a whirl of the wand!
SPRINKLE
Oh, oh! Let me try!
...potions were Aurora's biggest challenge.
PLUNK PLUNK
Water, weed, web, and wand--
WAIT!
BOOOM!

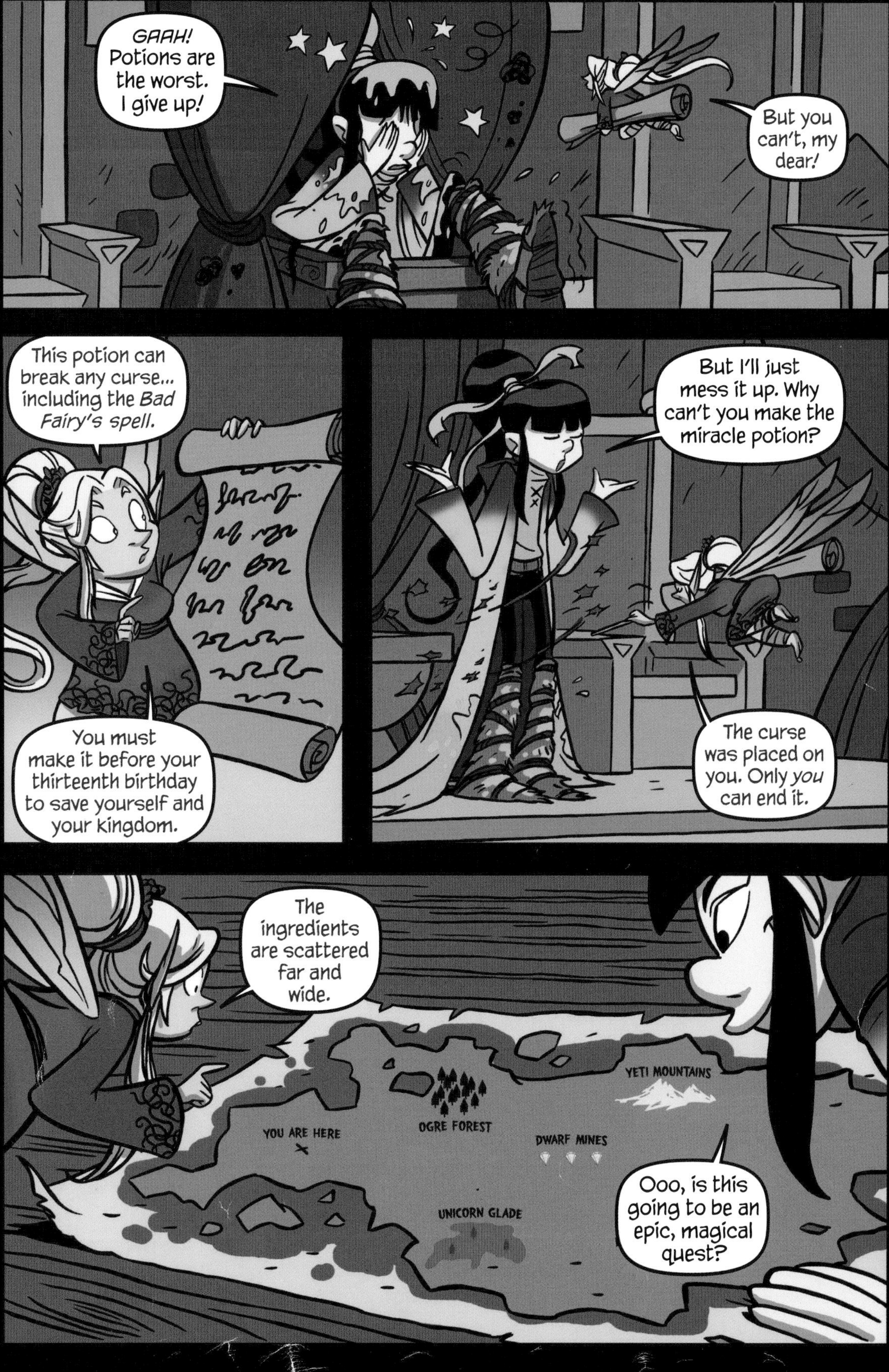
GAAH! Potions are the worst. I give up!
But you can't, my dear!
This potion can break any curse... including the *Bad Fairy's spell*.
You must make it before your thirteenth birthday to save yourself and your kingdom.
But I'll just mess it up. Why can't you make the miracle potion?
The curse was placed on you. Only *you* can end it.
The ingredients are scattered far and wide.
YETI MOUNTAINS
YOU ARE HERE
OGRE FOREST
DWARF MINES
UNICORN GLADE
Ooo, is this going to be an epic, magical quest?

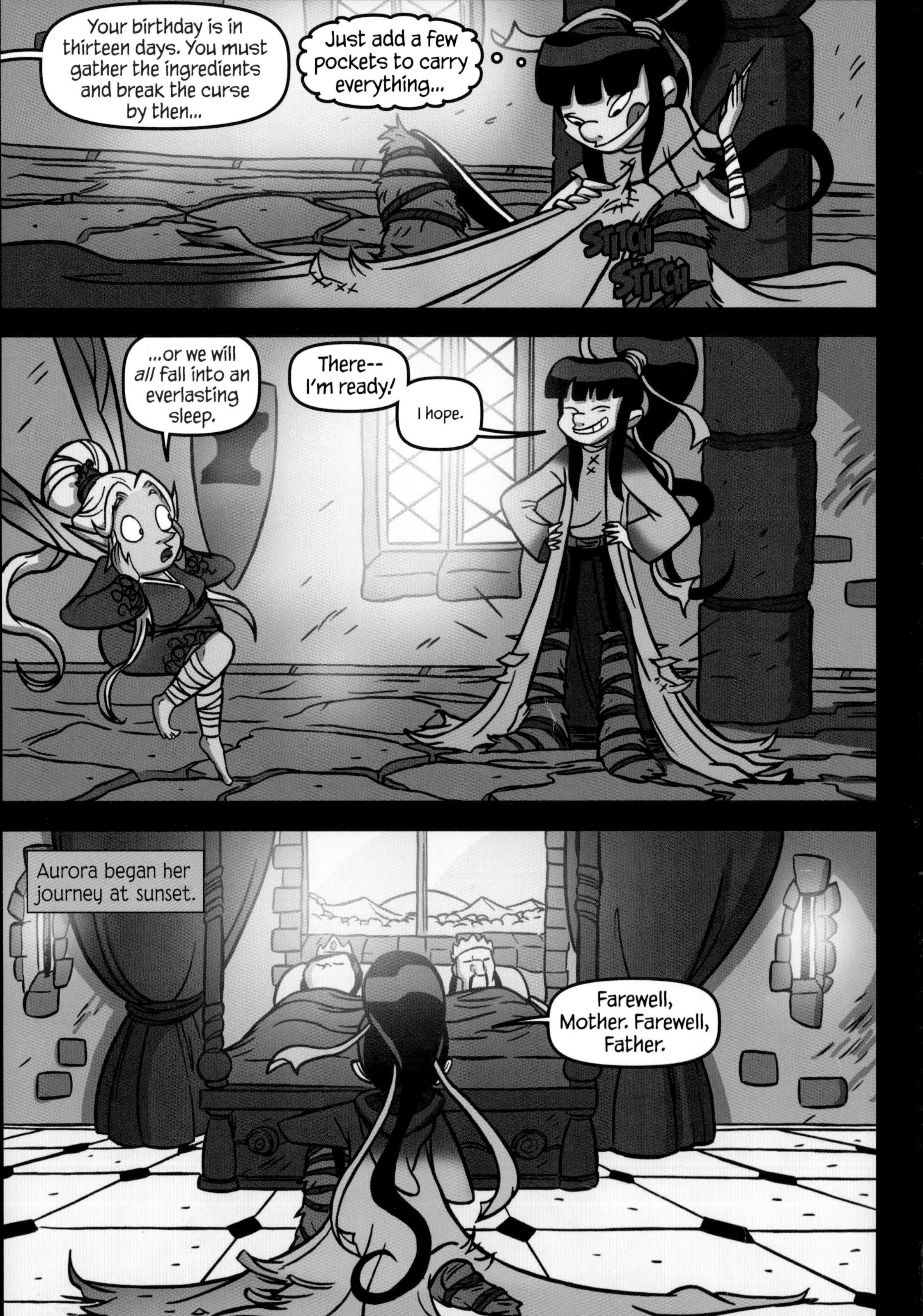
Your birthday is in thirteen days. You must gather the ingredients and break the curse by then...
Just add a few pockets to carry everything...
STITCH
STITCH
...or we will *all* fall into an everlasting sleep.
There-- I'm ready!
I hope.
Aurora began her journey at sunset.
Farewell, Mother. Farewell, Father.

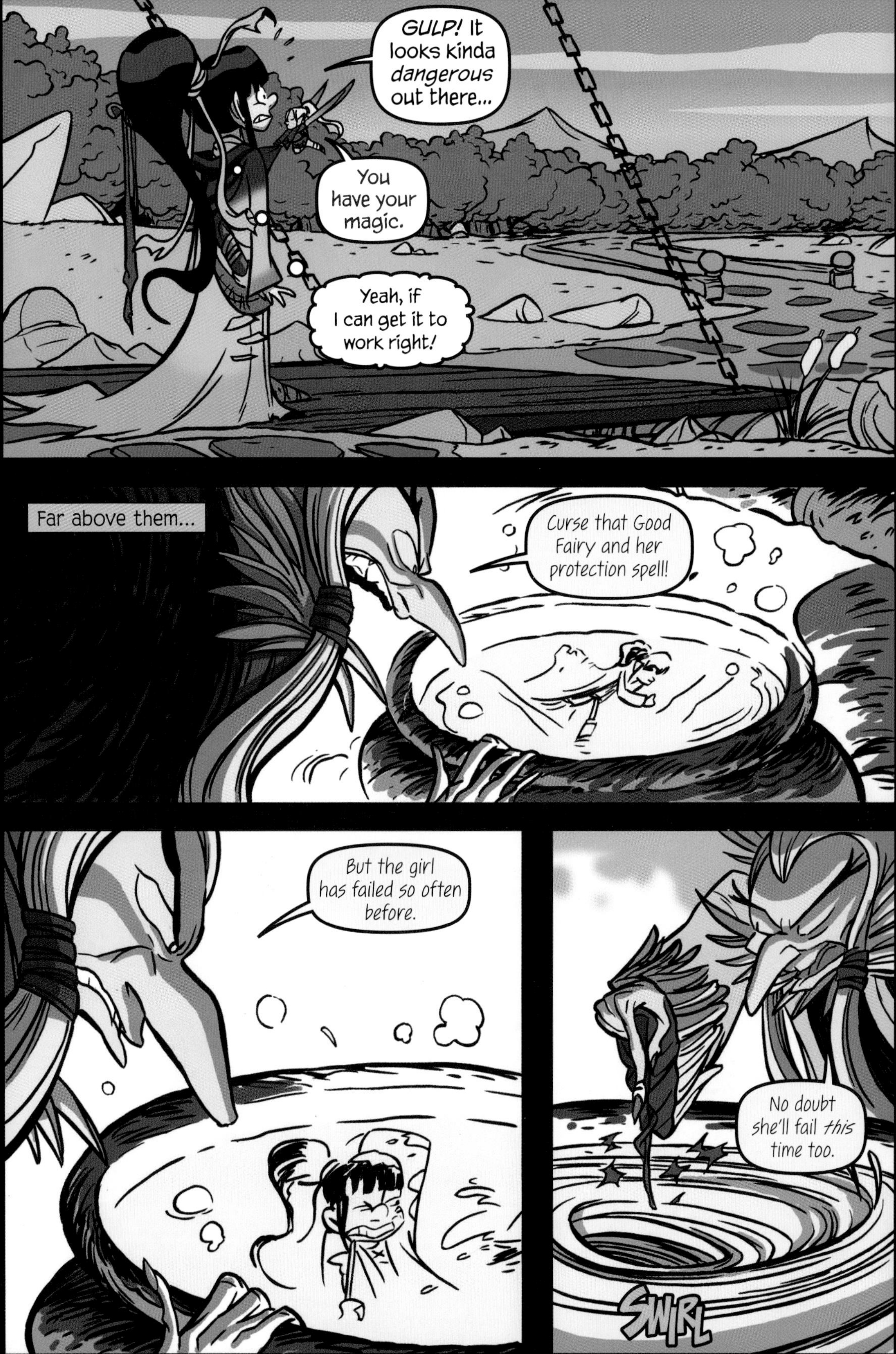
GULP! It looks kinda dangerous out there...
You have your magic.
Yeah, if I can get it to work right!
Far above them...
Curse that Good Fairy and her protection spell!
But the girl has failed so often before.
No doubt she'll fail this time too.
SWIRL

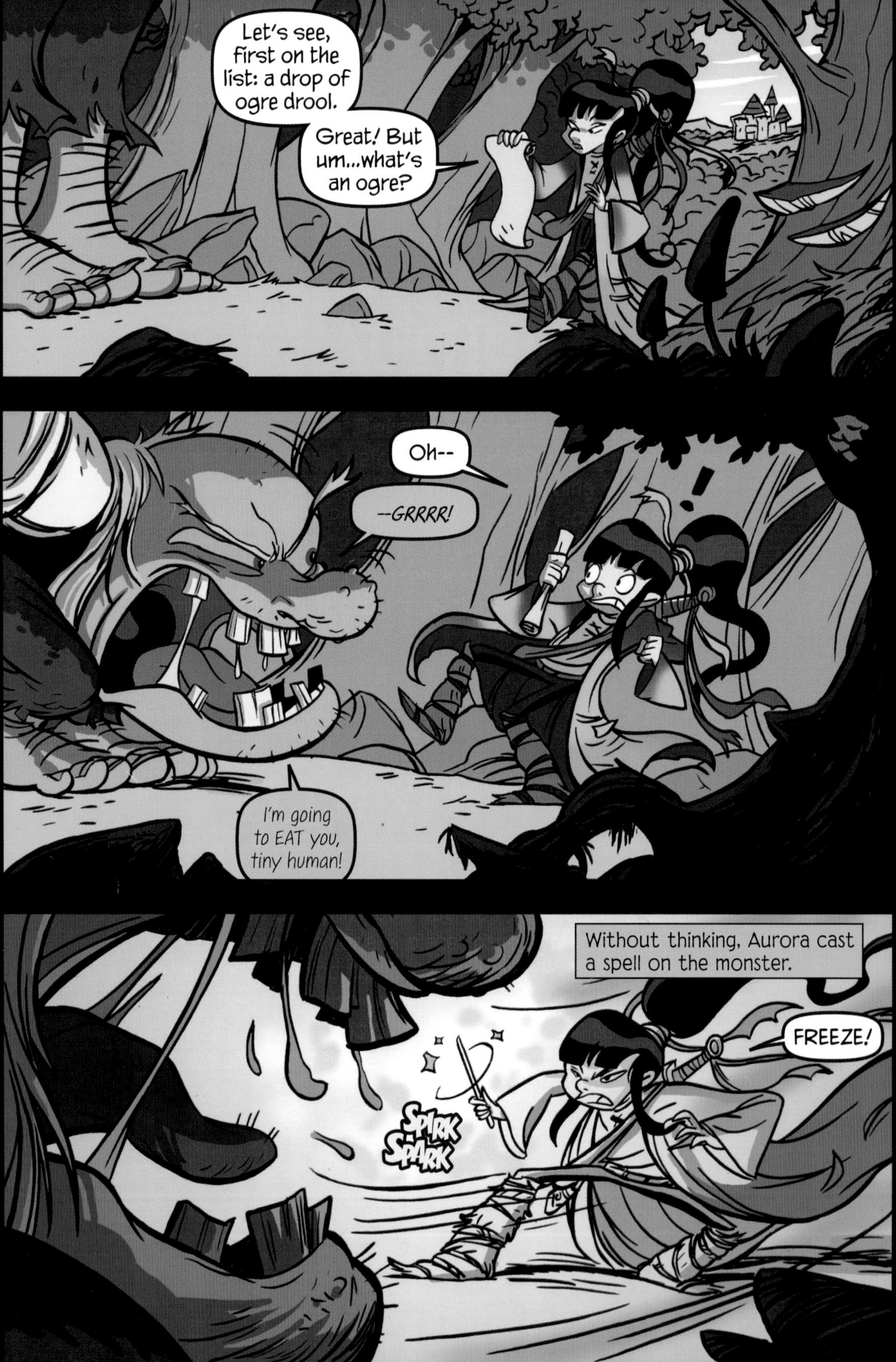
Let's see, first on the list: a drop of ogre drool.
Great! But um...what's an ogre?
Oh--
--GRRRR!
I'm going to EAT you, tiny human!
Without thinking, Aurora cast a spell on the monster.
FREEZE!
SPIRK SPARK

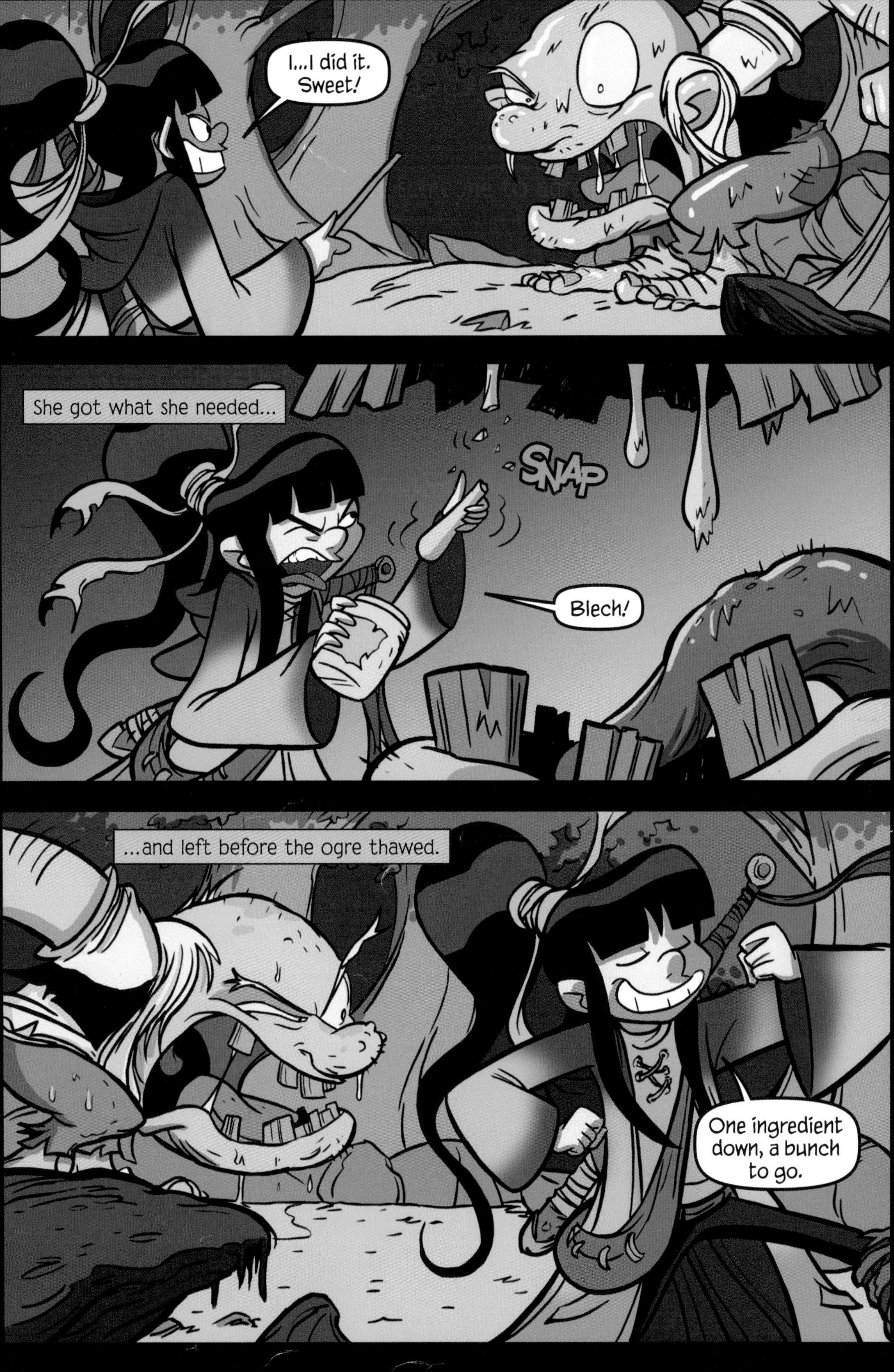
I...I did it. Sweet!
She got what she needed...
SNAP
Blech!
...and left before the ogre thawed.
One ingredient down, a bunch to go.

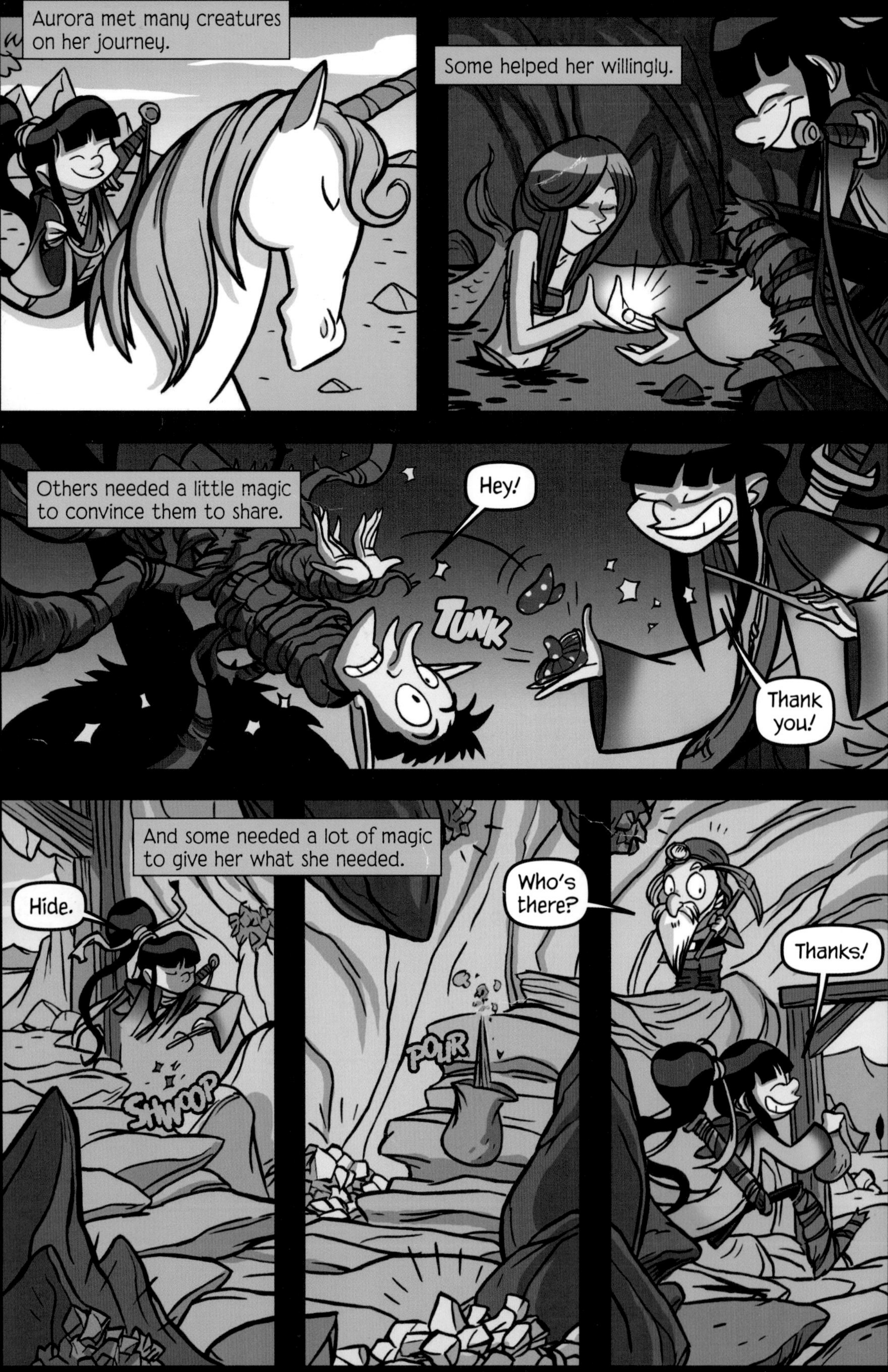
Aurora met many creatures on her journey.
Some helped her willingly.
Others needed a little magic to convince them to share.
Hey!
TUNK
Thank you!
And some needed a lot of magic to give her what she needed.
Hide.
SHWOOP
POUR
Who's there?
Thanks!

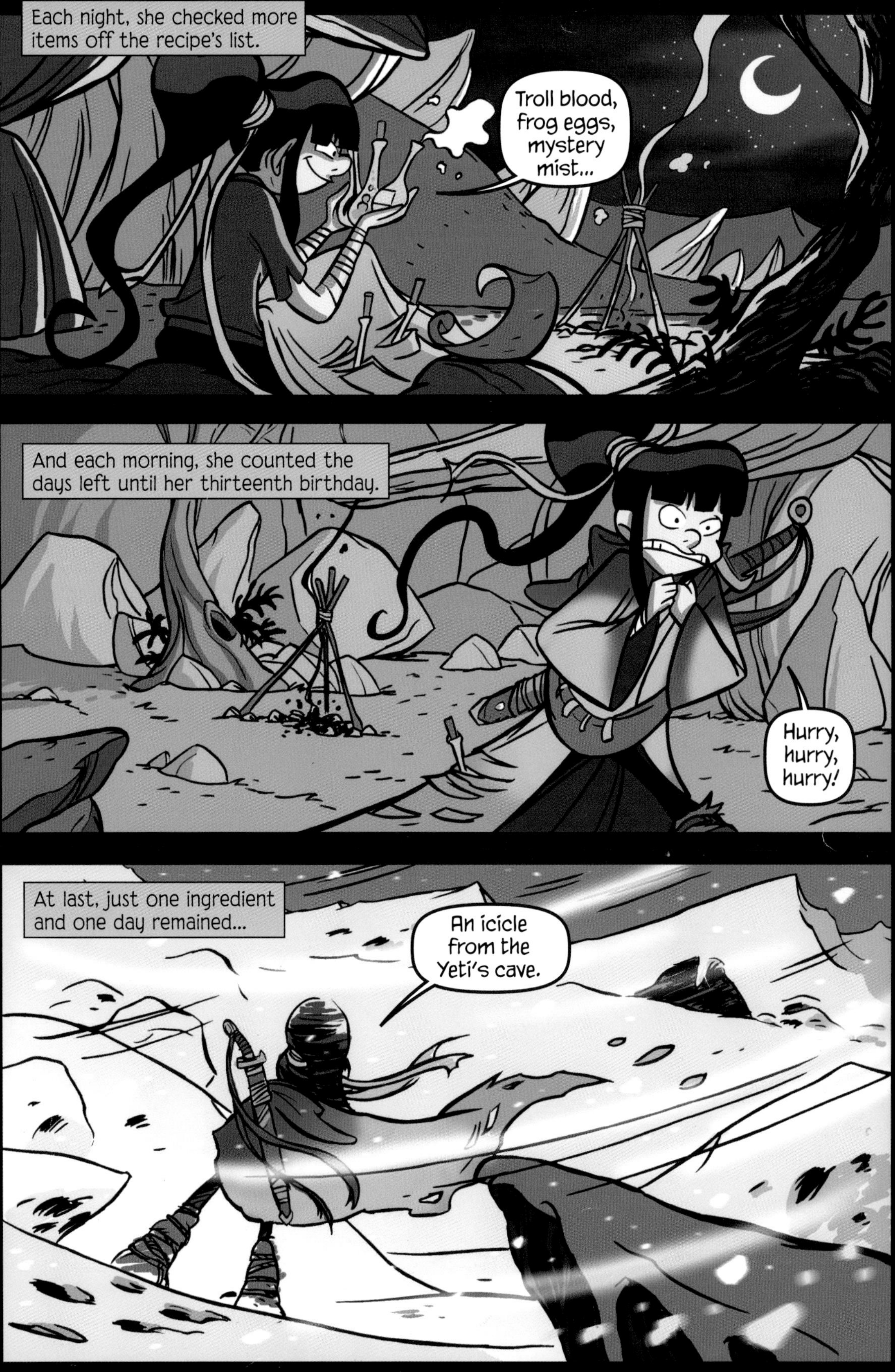
Each night, she checked more items off the recipe's list.
Troll blood, frog eggs, mystery mist...
And each morning, she counted the days left until her thirteenth birthday.
Hurry, hurry, hurry!
At last, just one ingredient and one day remained...
An icicle from the Yeti's cave.

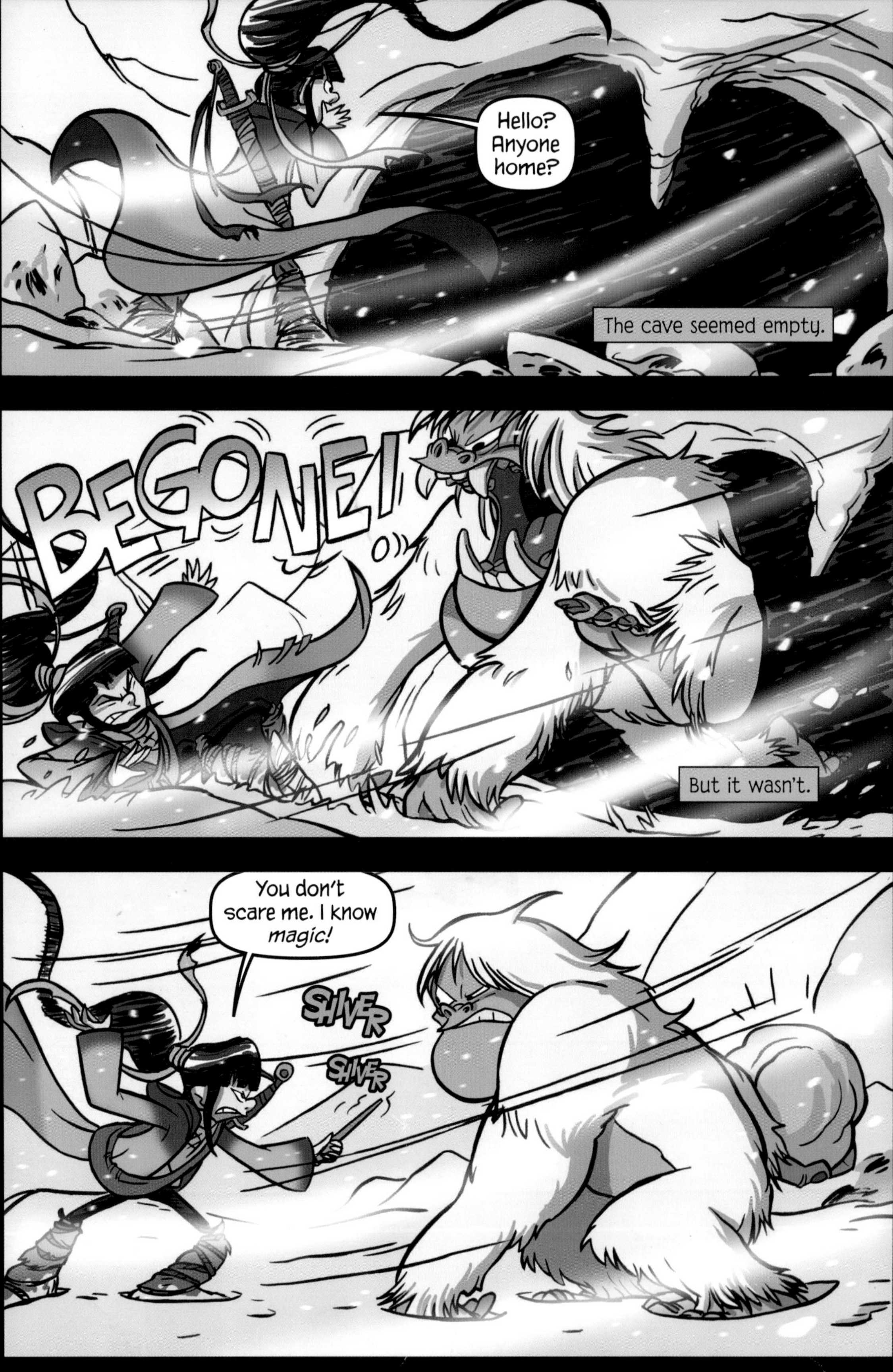
Hello? Anyone home?
The cave seemed empty.
BEGONE!
But it wasn't.
You don't scare me. I know *magic!*
SHIVER
SHIVER

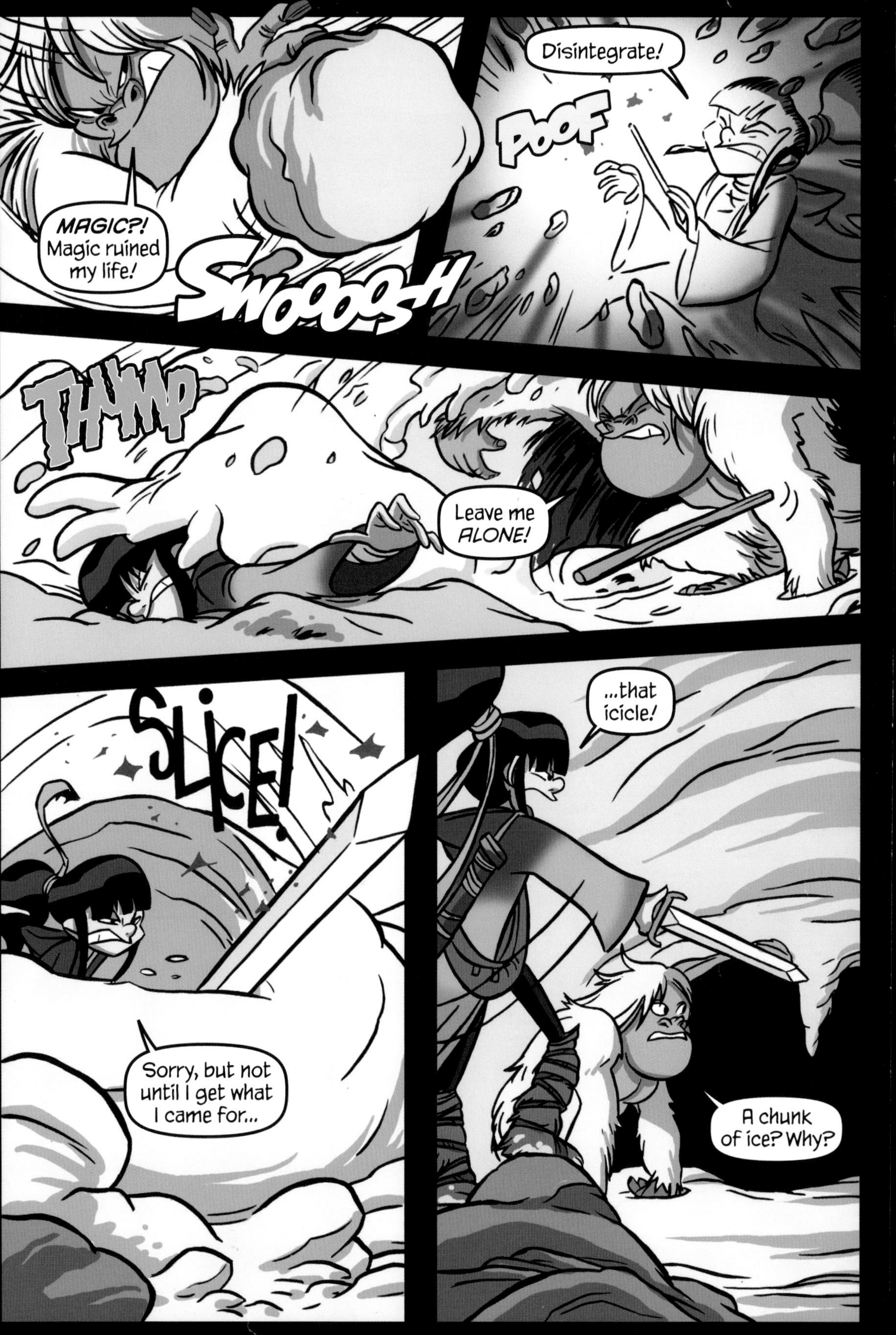
MAGIC?! Magic ruined my life!
SWOOOOSH
Disintegrate!
POOF
THUMP
Leave me ALONE!
SLICE!
Sorry, but not until I get what I came for...
...that icicle!
A chunk of ice? Why?

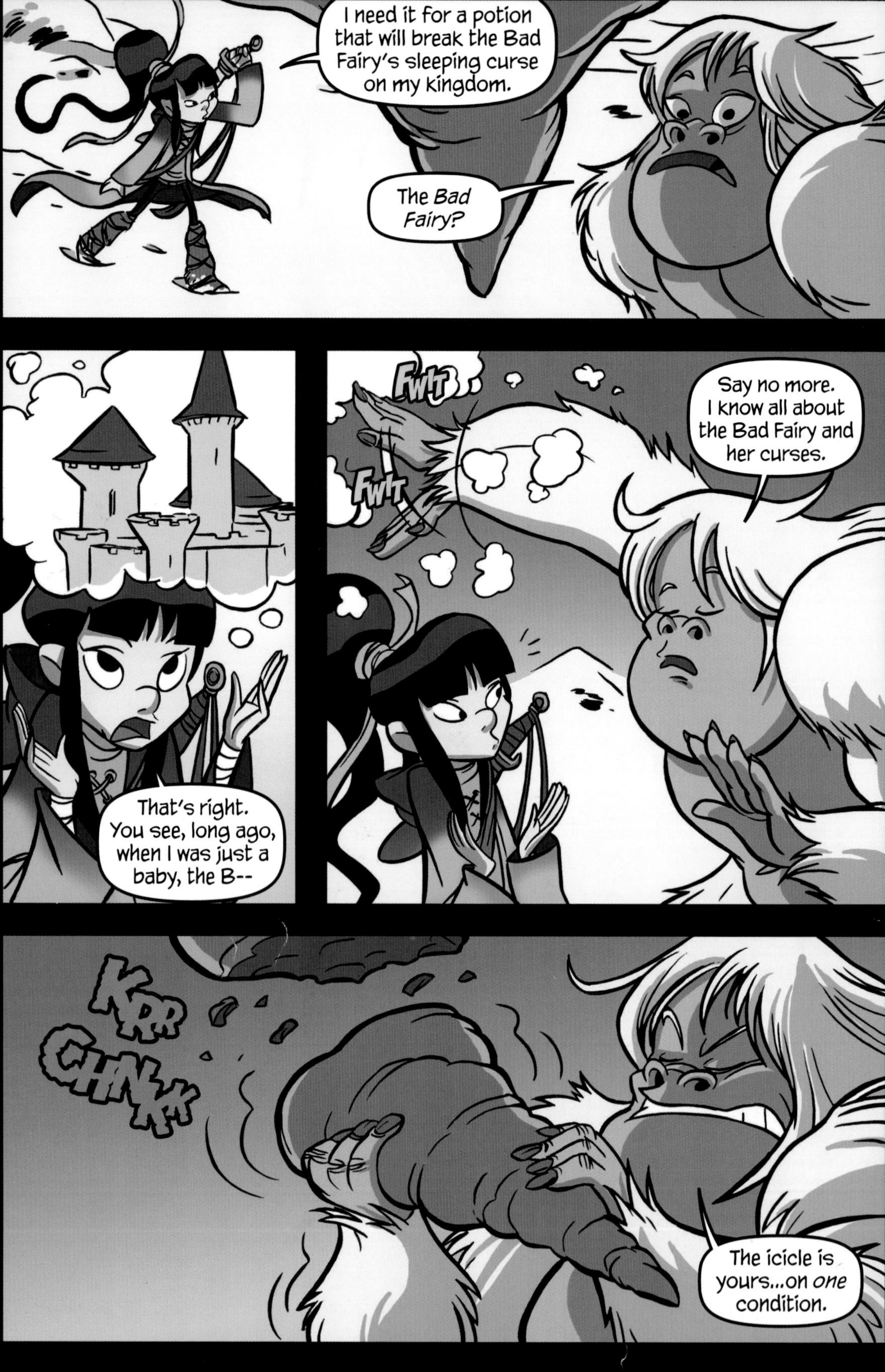

I need it for a potion that will break the Bad Fairy's sleeping curse on my kingdom.
The *Bad Fairy?*
That's right. You see, long ago, when I was just a baby, the B--
FWIT
FWIT
Say no more. I know all about the Bad Fairy and her curses.
KRR CHNKK
The icicle is yours...on *one* condition.

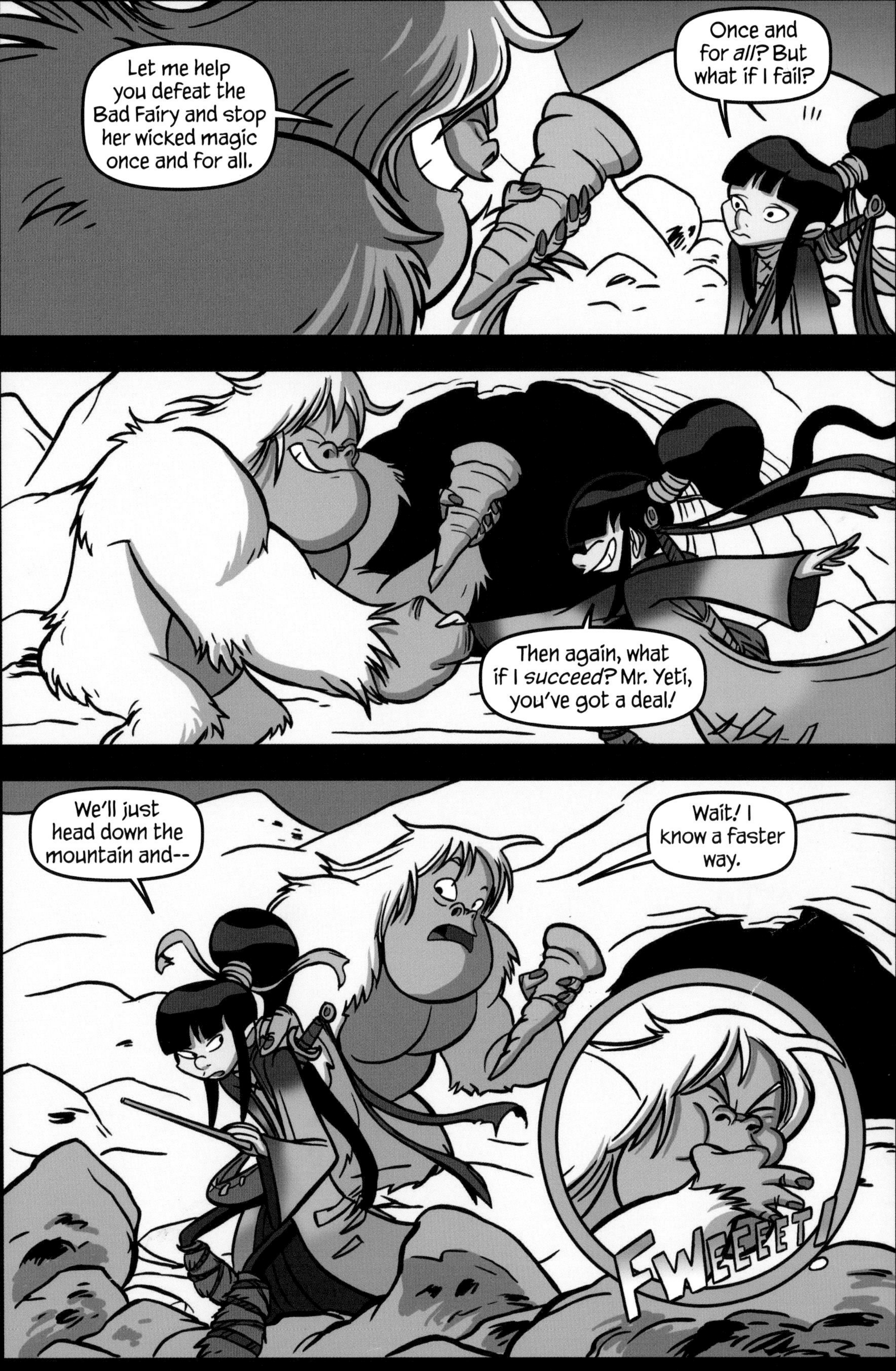

Let me help you defeat the Bad Fairy and stop her wicked magic once and for all.
Once and for *all*? But what if I fail?
Then again, what if I *succeed*? Mr. Yeti, you've got a deal!
We'll just head down the mountain and--
Wait! I know a faster way.
FWEEEET!

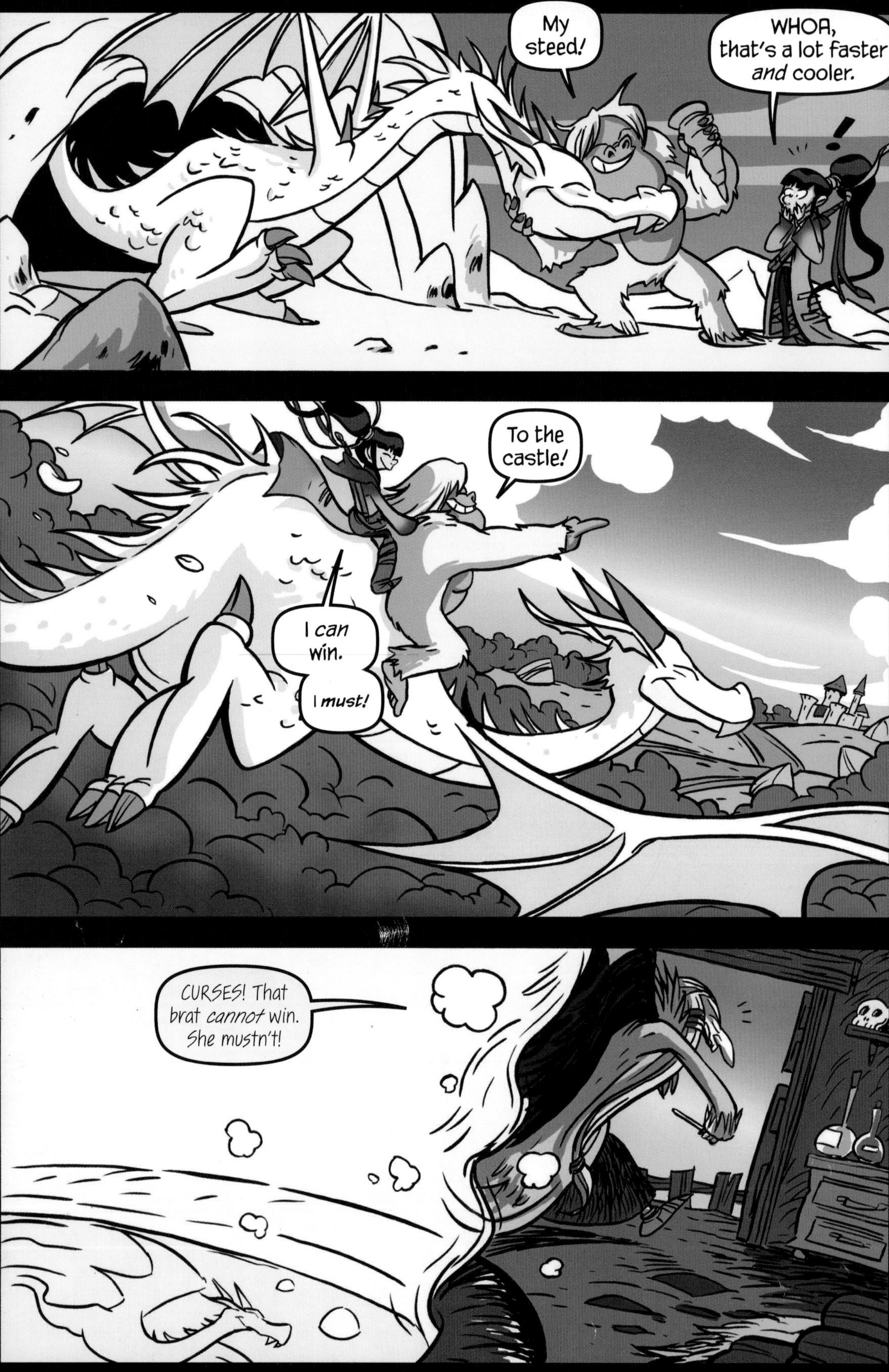
My steed!
WHOA, that's a lot faster *and* cooler.
!
To the castle!
I *can* win.
I *must!*
CURSES! That brat *cannot* win. She mustn't!

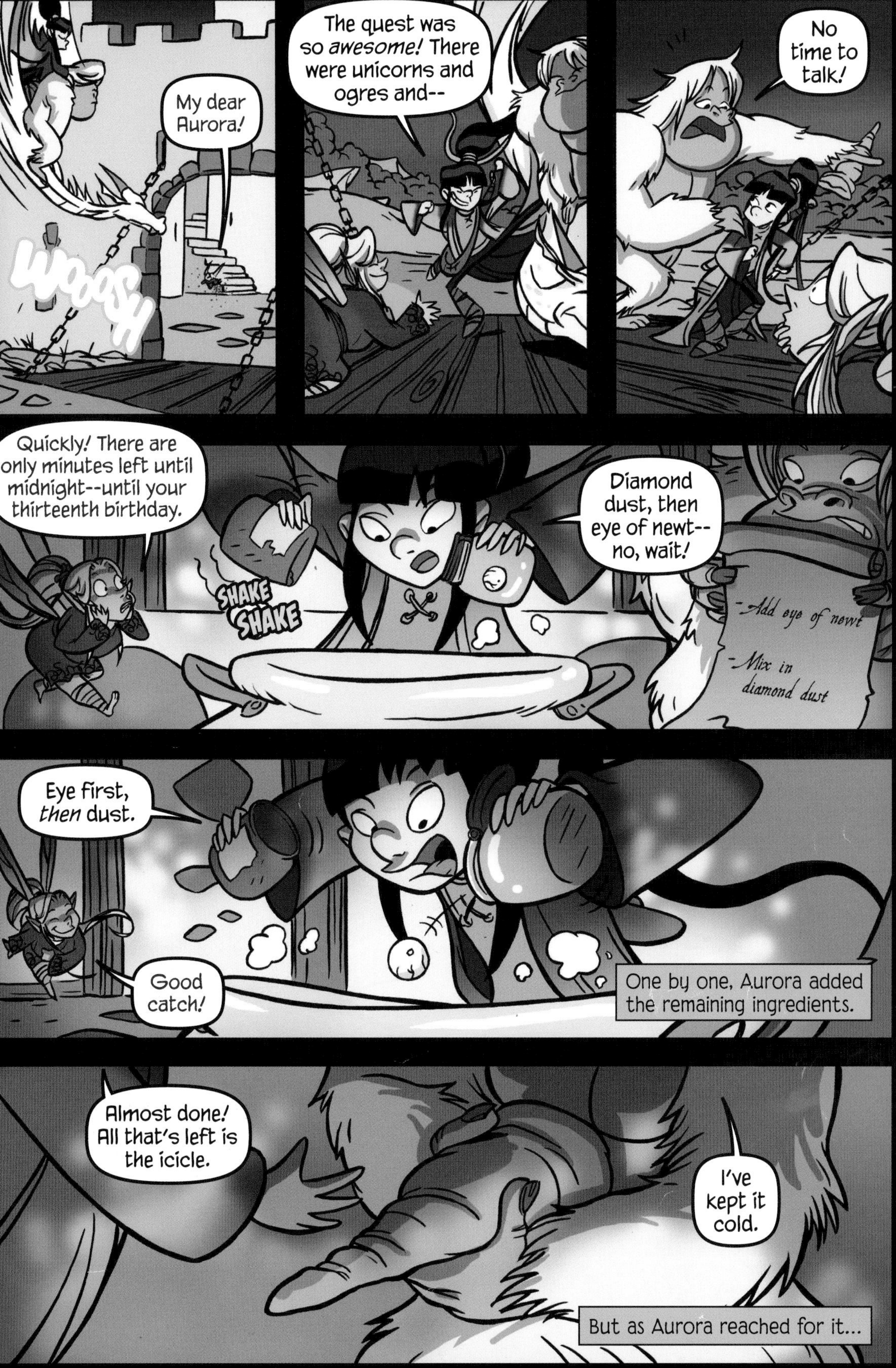
WOOOSH
My dear Aurora!
The quest was so *awesome!* There were unicorns and ogres and--
No time to talk!
Quickly! There are only minutes left until midnight--until your thirteenth birthday.
SHAKE SHAKE
Diamond dust, then eye of newt-- no, wait!
-Add eye of newt
-Mix in diamond dust
Eye first, *then* dust.
Good catch!
One by one, Aurora added the remaining ingredients.
Almost done! All that's left is the icicle.
I've kept it cold.
But as Aurora reached for it...

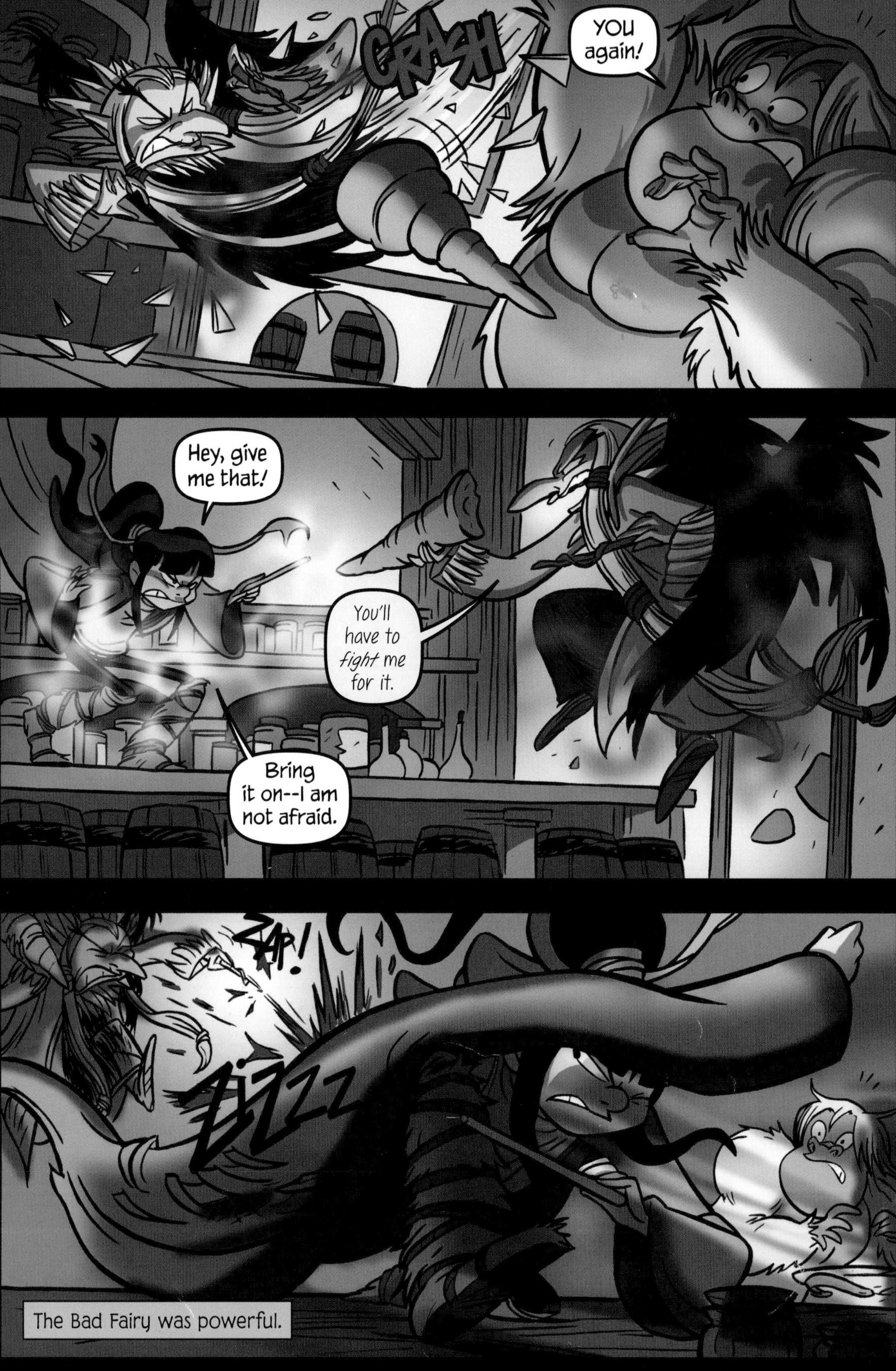
CRASH
YOU again!
Hey, give me that!
You'll have to *fight* me for it.
Bring it on--I am not afraid.
ZAP!
ZIZZZ
The Bad Fairy was powerful.

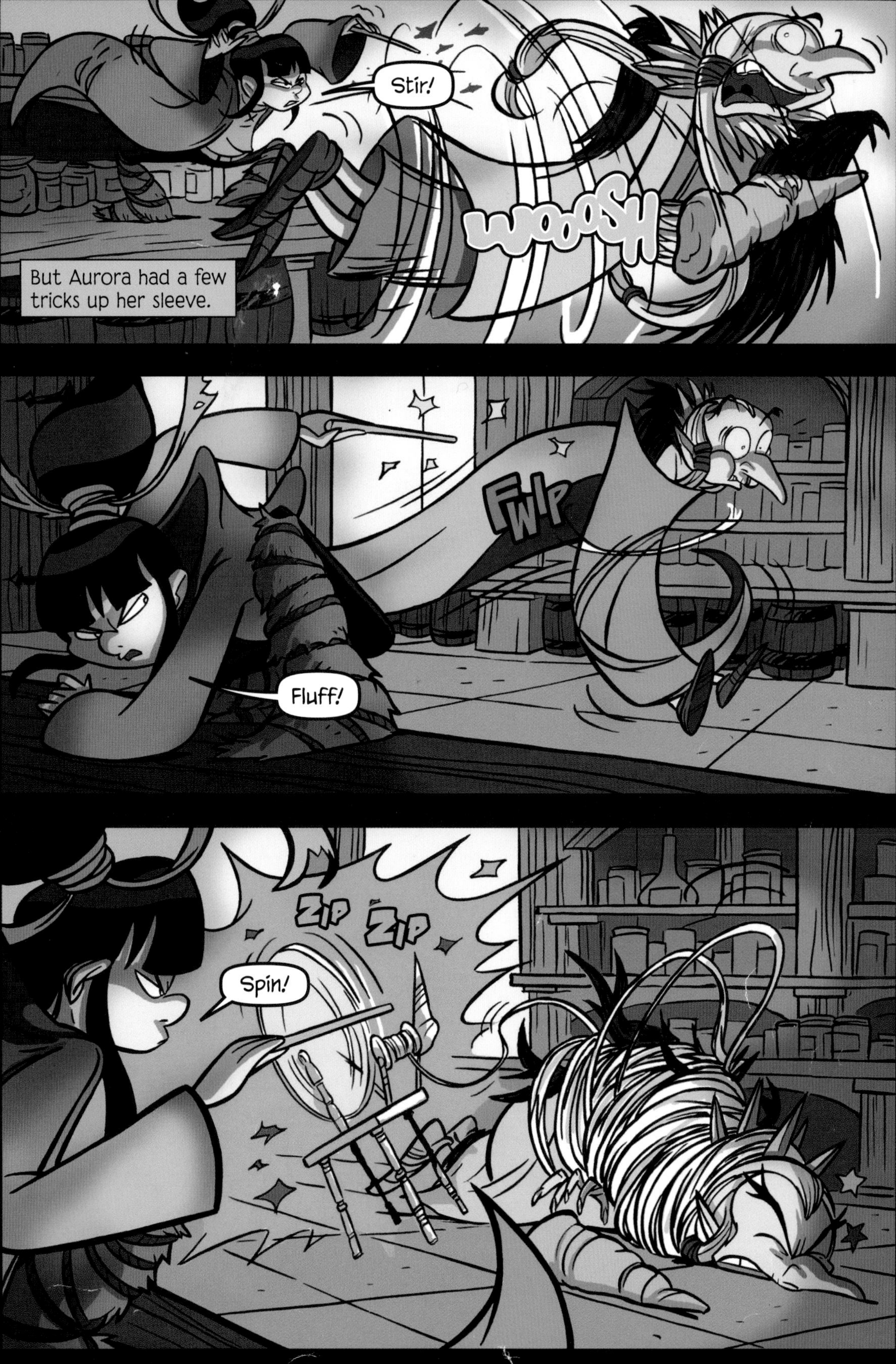
Stir!
WOOOOSH
But Aurora had a few tricks up her sleeve.
FWIP
Fluff!
ZIP ZIP
Spin!

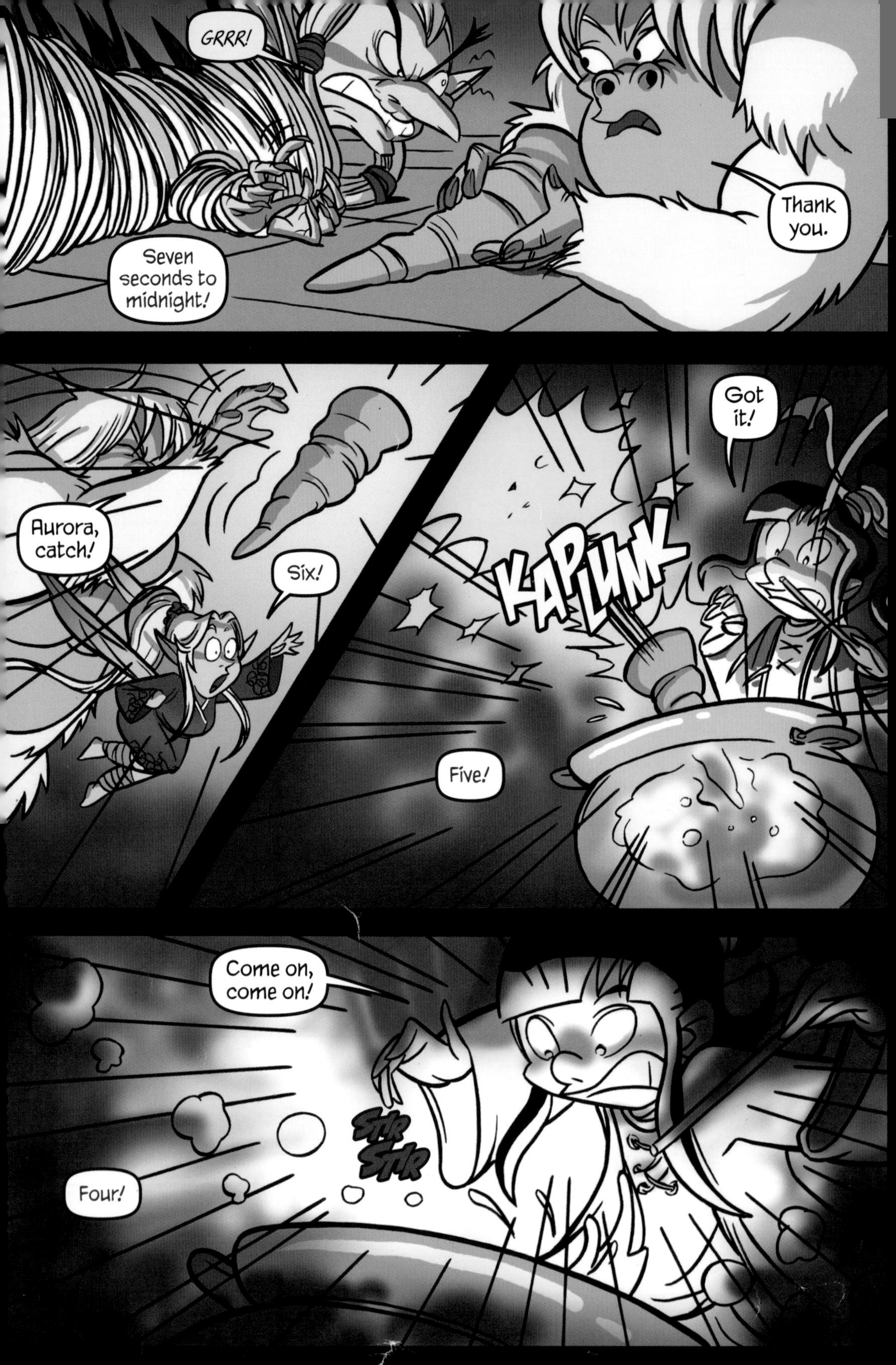
GRRR!
Seven seconds to midnight!
Thank you.
Aurora, catch!
Six!
Got it!
KAPLUNK
Five!
Come on, come on!
STIR STIR
Four!

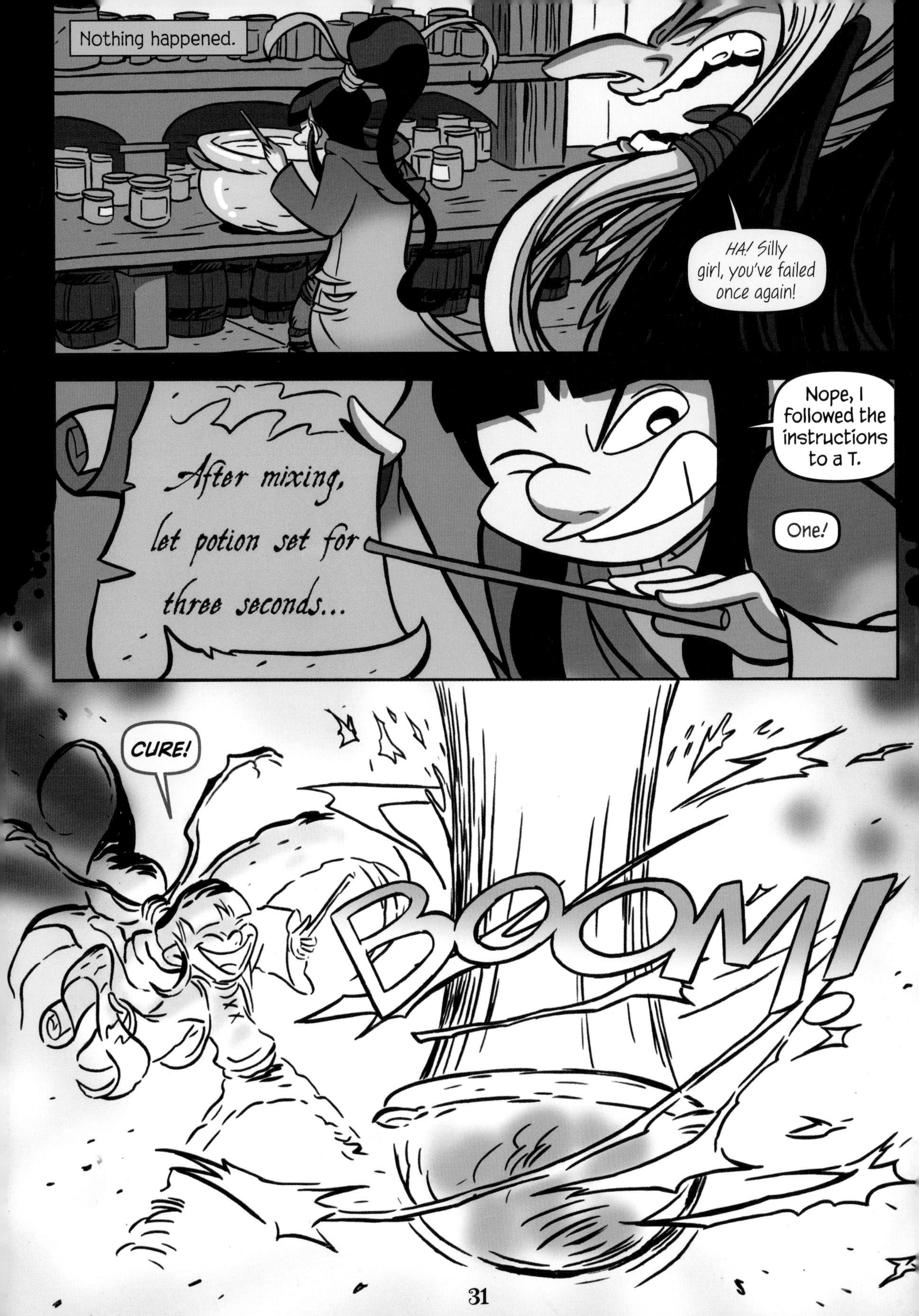

Nothing happened.
HA! Silly girl, you've failed once again!
Nope, I followed the instructions to a T.
After mixing, let potion set for three seconds...
One!
CURE!
BOOM!

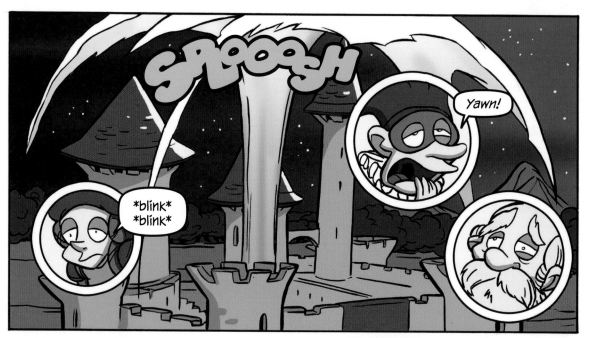

SROOSH

Yawn!

blink
blink

I did it!

Didn't I?

See for yourself.

Aurora!

Mother! Father!

AAAAHHH!

What a good nap.

Wait, Yeti?! Where are you?

Here!

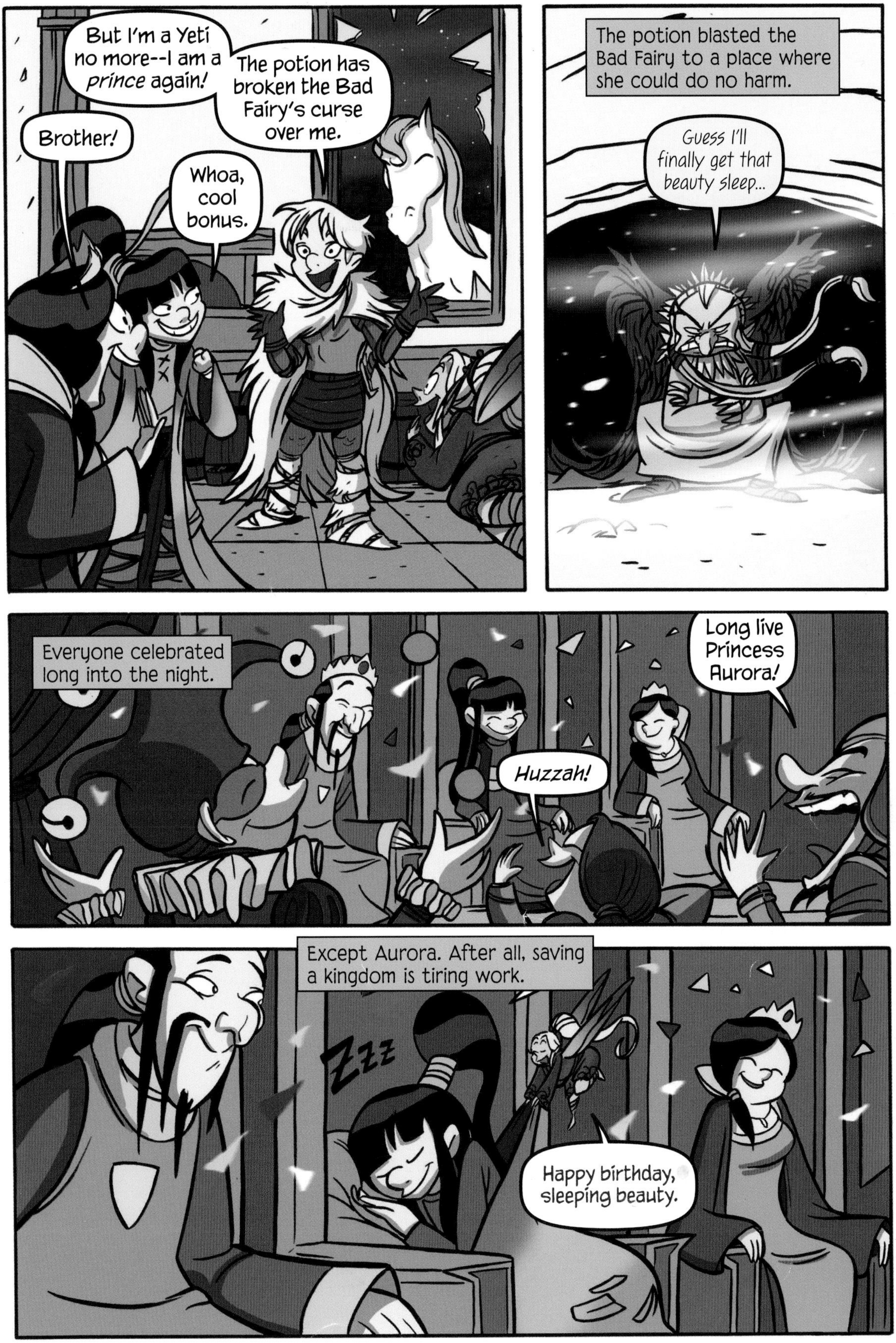
Brother!
But I'm a Yeti no more--I am a *prince* again!
The potion has broken the Bad Fairy's curse over me.
Whoa, cool bonus.
The potion blasted the Bad Fairy to a place where she could do no harm.
Guess I'll finally get that beauty sleep...
Everyone celebrated long into the night.
Huzzah!
Long live Princess Aurora!
Except Aurora. After all, saving a kingdom is tiring work.
ZZZ
Happy birthday, sleeping beauty.

ALL ABOUT THE ORIGINAL TALE!

Tales of a sleeping princess date back as early as 1528. Although none of them include a spell-casting heroine, they do include plenty of curses!

In the 1697 version by French storyteller Charles Perrault, seven fairies are invited to celebrate a princess's birth. As the feast begins, an eighth, older fairy arrives whom no one remembered to invite. Six of the fairies grant the baby gifts of beauty, grace, wit, dance, song, and music. The old fairy, angry over being forgotten, casts a curse--the princess shall prick her hand on a spindle and die. But the seventh good fairy still has her gift. She softens the curse. Instead of death, the princess will sleep for one hundred years.

Sixteen years pass. One day, the young princess finds an old woman in a tower using a spindle. This woman didn't know that the king had long ago forbidden spindles. The princess pricks her hand and falls into a deep slumber. The seventh fairy returns to the castle and puts the kingdom to sleep so the princess won't be alone when she wakes.

One hundred years later, a prince hears the legend of the sleeping princess. He finds his way to the castle and inside discovers the girl. Overcome with her beauty, he kneels beside her bed. Just then, the hundred-year enchantment ends and the princess awakens. (In the version by the Brothers Grimm, a kiss breaks the spell.) Soon after, the rest of the kingdom wakes, and the prince and princess marry.

Most retellings of Sleeping Beauty's tale end with that lovely picture. But Perrault's story has a second part. In it, the prince's mother is an ogress. The wicked ogress plots to cook and eat the young couple's son and daughter. When the ogress's plan is discovered, she throws herself into a vat of vipers. Happy ending indeed!

A FAR OUT GUIDE TO THE TALE'S MAGICAL TWISTS!

In the original tale, fairies bless the baby princess with special gifts, like beauty and grace. In this story, the Good Fairy gives Aurora awesome magic powers!

Instead of taking a hundred-year nap, Aurora goes on an epic quest to save her slumbering kingdom!

A kiss breaks the curse in the original story. But in this far-out version, a miracle potion made of the rarest ingredients saves the day!

Aurora doesn't lie around waiting for a prince to help her. Instead, she rescues a long-lost prince!

VISUAL QUESTIONS

1

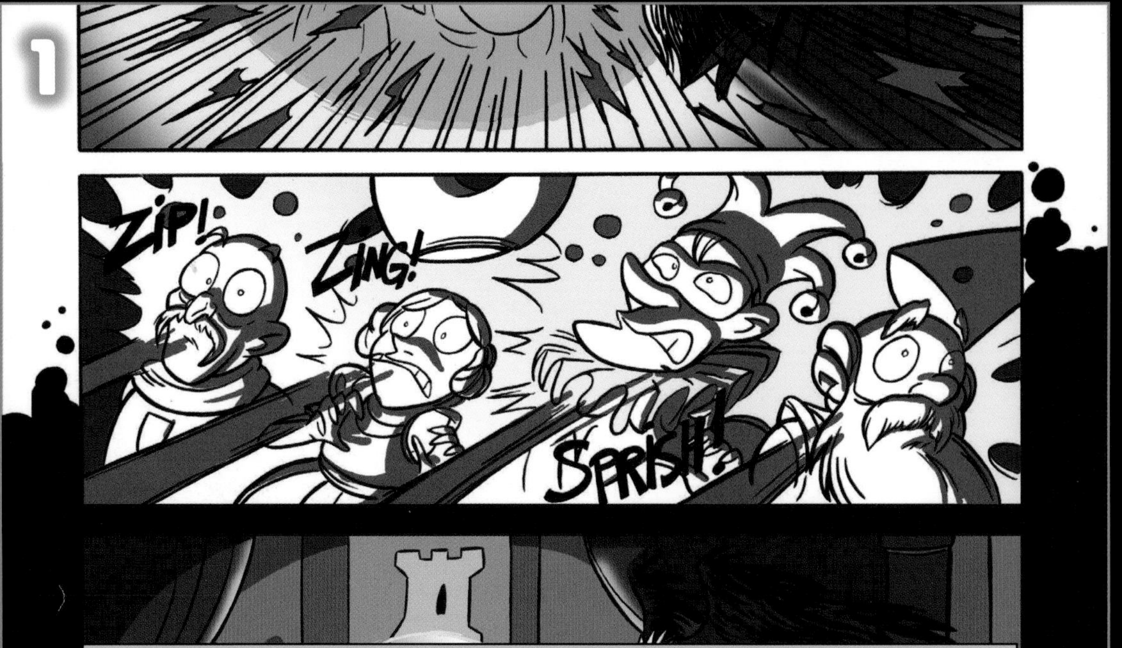
ZIP!
ZING!
SPRISH!

The space between comic panels is called the gutter. Why is the gutter turning from white to black? How does it connect to what's happening in the story? What happens to the gutter after page 31? Why?

2

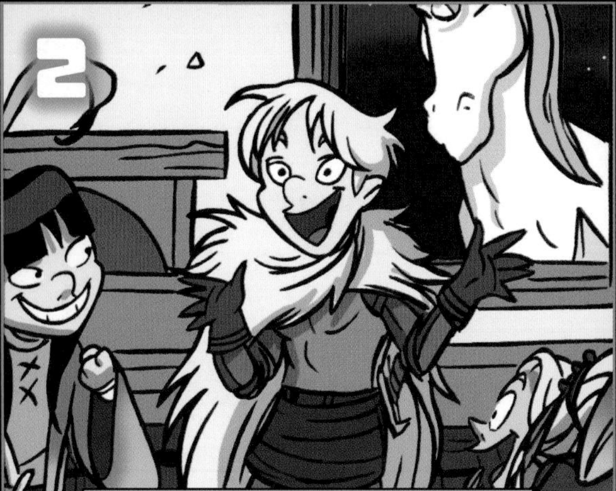

Were you surprised that the Yeti was really the long-lost prince? Look back through the story, and write down at least two text clues and two visual clues that hinted at this secret.

3

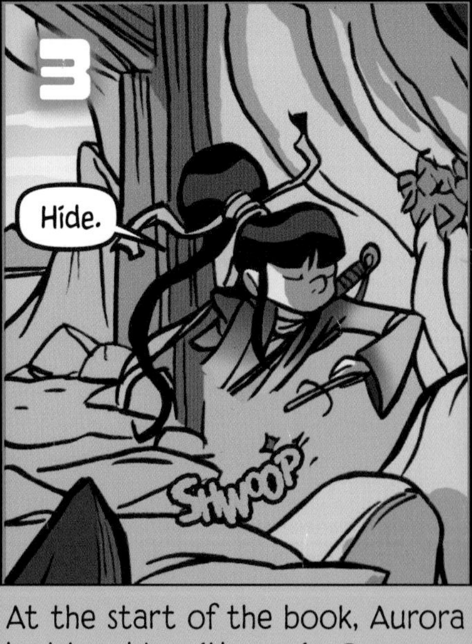
Hide.
SHWOOP

At the start of the book, Aurora had trouble with magic. Do you think she's a magic master now? Why or why not?

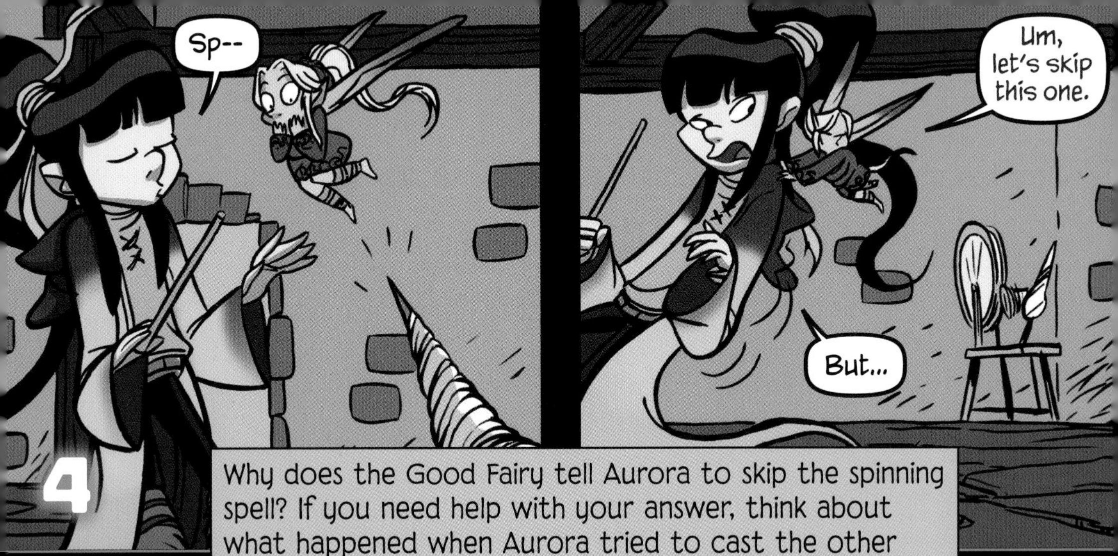
Sp--
Um, let's skip this one.
But...

4

Why does the Good Fairy tell Aurora to skip the spinning spell? If you need help with your answer, think about what happened when Aurora tried to cast the other spells, and also think about what happens in the original tale. Why do you think the creators included this scene?

What does the Bad Fairy think Aurora is feeling in this scene? How do you think Aurora is actually feeling? Talk about the reasons behind each of your answers.

5

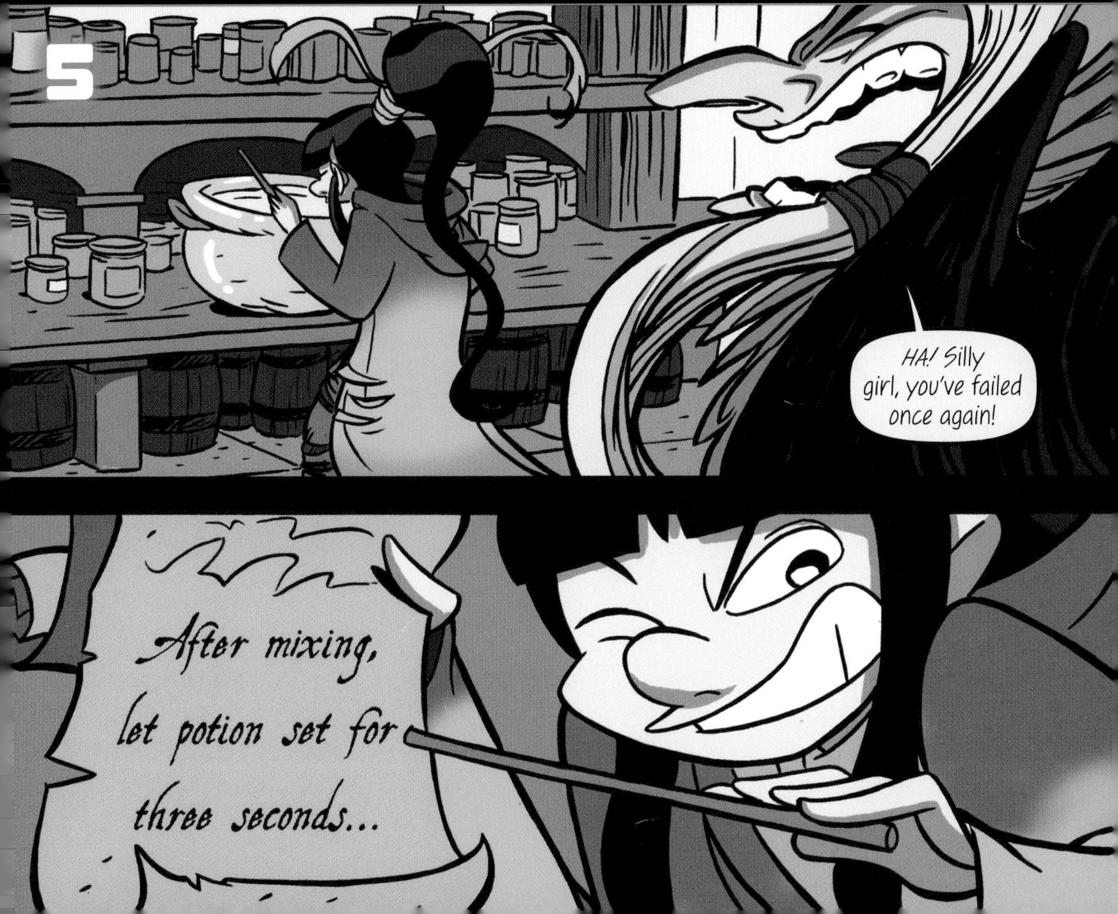
HA! Silly girl, you've failed once again!
After mixing, let potion set for three seconds...

AUTHOR

Stephanie True Peters worked as a children's book editor for ten years before she started writing books herself. She has since written forty books, including the New York Times best seller *A Princess Primer: A Fairy Godmother's Guide to Being a Princess*. When not at her computer, Peters enjoys playing with her two children, hitting the gym, or working on home improvement projects with her patient and supportive husband, Daniel.

ILLUSTRATOR

Alex Lopez became a professional illustrator and comic-book artist in 2001, but he's been drawing ever since he can remember. Lopez's pieces have been published in many countries, including the USA, UK, Spain, France, Italy, Belgium, and Turkey. He's also worked on a wide variety of projects from illustrated books to video games to marketing... but what he loves most is making comic books.

GLOSSARY

convince (kuhn-VINSS)--get someone to agree to do something

curse (KURS)--an evil spell meant to harm someone; to cast an evil spell

defeat (Di-FEET)--beat or win victory over something or someone, such as in a war, fight, or contest

disintegrate (dis-IN-tuh-greyt)--break up or destroy

disturb (diss-TURB)--bother or interrupt someone

ingredients (in-GREE-dee-uhnts)--items that are used to make something (like a miracle potion!)

potion (POH-shun)--a mixture that is meant to have special or magical effects

protection (proh-TEK-shuhn)--something that keeps a person or thing safe from harm

quest (KWEST)--a long, often difficult, journey made in order to find something

steed (STEED)--a fast horse (or dragon!) that a person rides

wicked (WIK-id)--very evil, bad, or mean

willingly (WIL-ing-lee)--when you do something willingly, you're happy and ready to do it

AWESOMELY EVER AFTER.

FAR OUT FAIRY TALES